# Cascades

*General Editor:* Geoff Fox

# My Mate Shofiq

Titles in the *Cascades* series include:

### The Man with Eyes like Windows      Gareth Owen
Louie's dad has been an actor and a songwriter – his was
the walk-on part, and other people's names are on his
songs. He's a drifter, forever leaving his children in search
of fame. This is the story of his son's quest to bring him
home.

### The Stone Book Quartet   Alan Garner
Four stories interconnected which weave together time
and place, skills and secrets to make up the texture of a
family's life in different generations.

### Tough Luck      Berlie Doherty
Joe Bead, third year tutor gets on well with his class.
However, he is having a problem getting through to
Twagger, a sullen absentee. He's also worried about
Nasim, just arrived from Pakistan, who is feeling very
friendless and very foreign.

### Why the Whales Came      Michael Morpurgo
Recently made into a film, this book is set on the island of
Samson, where the Birdman, Gracie and Daniel discover a
whale stranded on the beach. To the islanders, the whale is
theirs to kill. To stop them and lift the curse on the island
forever the Birdman has to reveal his secret.

### The Coal House      Andrew Taylor
Alison is 13. Her mother has recently died and, her Dad has
just bought a house 300 miles away from the world she
knows. Brimming with resentment, she is determined to
dislike the rambling old Coal House. But the house has an
unsolved mystery which draws her in.

# My Mate Shofiq

## Jan Needle

CollinsEducational
*An imprint of* HarperCollins*Publishers*

© Jan Needle, 1978

ISBN 0 00 330005 6

First published by André Deutsch Ltd, 1978
Published in *Cascades* in 1983 by Collins Educational
Reprinted 1987, 1990, 1991
Printed in Great Britain by Martins of Berwick

*For Buf and Hughie*

# Chapter One

To be quite honest, Bernard hadn't been thinking about trouble that morning. Although it was cold – as cold as charity, whatever that meant – his mind hadn't been thinking about real things much at all. He'd had a problem with his submarine the night before, and he was turning it over and over in his head as he wandered along Middleton Road. Bernard didn't usually bother with his submarine during the day, because it was very much a bed thing, but since his dad had told him that a petrol engine wouldn't work in a sub, because of using up the air, he'd been worrying. He might have to redesign it, quick, or invent a new type of engine. And meanwhile, England might lose the war.

That would be terrible, and as he waited to get across (Bernard always avoided the lollipop man, because he thought it was soft to cross at crossings) he considered the state of the battle before Dad's bombshell about engines. He'd been doing very well. He'd destroyed eleven German battleships, and one Russian, and he'd been lying on the seabed waiting for the sub-chaser to get near enough to be blasted with his special self-guiding torpedo. If he could have sewn up this part of the Atlantic, swept it clear of the enemy, he'd have been ready to sail for the Indian Ocean, where there was big trouble brewing.

He saw a gap in the traffic and darted out to the middle. There was a fair amount of slush on the road, and the lorries that passed sprayed him with cold damp. He saw one driver, high in his cab, mouth something at him, in an angry way. But a lady in a Morris 1000 stopped for him, and he ran to the other pavement.

He was wettish, and chilly up his legs below his anorak, so Bernard decided to run up New Earth Street and round the top of the croft. That way he'd warm up, and he still wouldn't be late. It was there, two hundred yards off the main road, that he saw Whitehead and his lot.

At first, Bernard stopped. He'd decided, without even thinking about it, to change tack entirely. If he nipped down Cobden Street, past the Musicians, he could get back on to Middleton Road and down to school. He wouldn't get his run in probably, but he wouldn't get his head punched either. Bobby Whitehead was a twerp, but he wasn't half a bully. And he had three of his lads, the little-'uns, with him, and that Pat Broome, that looked like the south end of a cow walking north. She was the roughest of the lot, except for Bobby himself.

He'd stuck his hands in his anorak, and pointed himself towards Cobden Street ('Thirty degrees of port helm on, sir', because he was a destroyer just at that moment) when he changed his mind again. Bobby Whitehead and his gang weren't looking his way at all, and they were behaving sort of funny. They looked as if they were stalking someone. He stood there, his breath steaming, his feet frozen in their soaking plimsoll-boots. He hunched his shoulders into his neck, he narrowed his eyes and glared along New Earth Street. He became Bernard of the Black Hand.

After a hundred yards or so, it became obvious that Bobby Whitehead's lot were looking for someone definite. They were going dead slow, despite the cold, and they were slinking along like Russian spies. They never looked behind them, which was good, because it made Bernard's task dead easy and dead safe. He nipped from doorway to doorway, dodging past fed-up people slouching off to work, and soon got pretty close. Close enough to see that Bobby and Pat, and at least one of the others, were carry-

8

ing bricks. They were out to bash someone. Bernard the Black Hand smiled a sneering smile. Little did they know that an enemy agent had them in his grasp. He patted the Luger under his left armpit. Once let them strike, that's all! Just one false move!

When they got to the edge of the waste ground, where the Jericho Mill had been till three months ago, the gang stopped. Bernard crept up a few feet to the alley round the boarded-up terrace, ran along to the other end, climbed the half-ruined garage wall and looked over at them. They were stopped, dead still, waiting. He saw little Georgie Greenwood speak, and Pat tell him to shut up – he saw the clouds of breath. He settled down to wait. He could guess now who they were planning on battering up. It was good fun, he liked to see a battering, as long as it wasn't him that was getting it.

There was a fair space of derelict ground between the old terrace and the wire fence round the school. It was good for playing, because the blokes who'd knocked down Jericho had left up lots of little bits of old wall, some of them quite high. The kids had all been warned off playing there, because it was meant to be dangerous, but that was barmy. Anyway, lots of kids lived in places where the waste ground was a short cut. Although they were meant to come along the roads – the school rules were always getting jammed down their throats about that – it was just stupid. Who'd walk a million miles to get to somewhere you could see just across the manky grass?

A lot of the kids that came straight across the waste ground were the Pakistanis, because they mostly lived down the Brook. This was an area that had once been quite posh, with great big old houses along the main roads and smaller brick terraces round behind them. They had high front doors, the big ones, and coloured glass porches. In the old days, when he'd just been a kid, Bernard remembered going down there quite a lot, on his way to the park and the rec. But it was all blackie-land now, and they only went down the Brook in big gangs, or with grown-ups. It was dead dangerous, that's for sure.

Sure enough though, that's what Bobby Whitehead was waiting for. As Bernard the Black Hand peered over the ruined wall, trying to breathe light, to stop his steaming breath giving him away, he could see Patsy Broome pointing. He followed her finger. Over the croft, along by what was left of the Jericho outside wall, was a gang of kids. They were white – one of them looked like his mate Maureen McIlroy in fact – but behind them there was a gaggle in pyjamas and other daft gear. Any second now Bobby and Co would set to stalking.

Bernard pondered on the subject of Pakistanis for a bit, but not in a serious way. His eyes and nose were running, and he reckoned that if he was cold, in jeans, two jumpers and his anorak with the real fur-trimmed hood, that lot must be freezing brass monkeys. They ought to feel it more, by rights, being as how they came from a hot country, or their mums and dads did, but there they were, quite plain now, in sort of silky trousers and smock-things, some of them. Nuts. Even the ones in ordinary gear didn't have anoraks on, just coats, not half so good. He wondered what the Whitehead lot would do to them.

As the gang came creeping past him, Bernard the Black Hand ducked down behind the wall. He patted his Luger again, although he knew he wouldn't be using it this morning. After all, it wasn't his fight, and he had no objection if Bobby and Pat wanted to bung a few bricks at the curry kids. That pair could be a menace, it wasn't safe to play anywhere they were around, and even the little'uns like they had with them today were pretty tough. His mate Mickie would have seen them off, all of them. But that was all over now.

He shook off thoughts of dead Mickie as the gang clattered past. They were a noisy lot, hopeless at tracking, not a patch on him. He grinned and slipped out after them. They took the school side of the next derelict terrace, he went behind. By the time they'd got along its length he was already hidden, waiting for them. He had a good view of the whole of that part of the croft, the part where the fight would be. Fight! He grinned again. Battering more like. Them poor little kids would get a right hammering; they didn't stand a chance.

Now he was closer, he could see them clearly. There were seven or eight of them, and they were very small, about four or six, that's all. He vaguely thought he recognised a couple of them, but then they all looked the same really, so he wasn't that sure. There were two little girls out front, holding hands, then a gap, then a knot of jabbering boys, then a couple more girls. Close to, he could make out that they had on jerseys under their pyjama-things. Not as green as they were cabbage-looking then; but they still looked ruddy cold.

The white kids who'd been near them had raced off towards the fence by now, and the rest were at the Whiteheads' mercy. For a moment Bernard switched sides in his head. He was with them, a lone waggon-train going across the Wild West prairies. He'd been out scouting for redskins, and on coming back to the main body of explorers he'd found a band about to attack. What should he do? Could he beat them single-handed, or should he gallop down to the waggons, form them in a circle, and prepare to fight off the attacking Indians? He almost laughed out loud. A band of Indians attacking that lot! They *were* Indians! Well it was different, at least – a waggon-train of Indians being attacked by a band of cowboys!

The Pakistani kids were just coming into good brick-bunging range, and he'd seen Whitehead's lot getting up a nice pile of good-size rocks to fling, when Bernard caught a movement out of the corner of his eye, away over to his right. He looked round, risking missing the first shot of the war, to see if he could pick it out.

Over that way it was a right jumble of old, half-down

houses, the beginnings of a new estate, and the ruins of another mill, the Muscovy, that still had some bits of old wrecked weaving machines in it. Bernard stared, into the wind, with his eyes watering badly. He'd almost given up, decided he'd been mistaken, when he saw it again. There *was* someone, someone hiding among the remains of the third terrace along, and creeping towards him.

He flicked his eyes from the shape, to the victims, to the Whiteheads. He squeezed his frozen finger-ends into his eyes to get the tears out, to get a clearer view. One of the little kids out front began to giggle at something, high and squeaky. Pat Broome weighed up a stone in her hand; she'd soon put a stop to that!

The figure along the way moved from behind an old outside lav, full into Bernard's view. He knew him! He was in the same class! It was a bloke called Shofiq, or something. Shofiq Rahman, or something. The two little girls who'd looked familiar clicked. They were his sisters, all dressed up in silk pyjamas while Shofiq wore jeans and a jumper. Blimey – even in this weather he never had a coat on, just jeans and a jumper.

Bernard watched with extra interest, because he knew Shofiq. Not to talk to, of course, because he didn't talk much, not even in class, when Miss told him to. He was very quiet, and very dark brown, and he had a funny smell to him, like an Indian restaurant, like all the Pakis. But he'd thumped some lad once, not so long ago, and none of the kids that liked to bash up the blackies ever touched him. He couldn't take on Bobby Whitehead though, that was obvious. Bobby Whitehead was the champ, he was an ace fighter.

Bernard felt very excited, his chest got tight. This lad was coming along fast now, and he had a dirty great wallbrick in his mitt.

Suddenly there was a big row. He looked back over the wall in time to see Bobby Whitehead, and Patsy Broome, and the three little'uns, all leap out from their hidey-hole and start bunging bricks. The air was full of them, and the little Pakistani kids just stood there for something like ages, with the rocks flying past their ears and bouncing off the soggy ground all round them. It was a miracle that none of them got hit, but they didn't seem to have the sense to do anything about it. Bernard the Black Hand almost forgot he was only there as a spy. He very nearly leapt up and yelled at them to run.

Bobby Whitehead and his lot were yelling all right, though. And they started to move slowly forward as they kept up the bombardment of stones. Some of the little kids started to dart about, as if they didn't know which way to turn. Bernard saw a rock bounce off the shoulder of a little girl of about five, and she fell into the cold mud, crying. Another little girl bent down to try and help her, with her long black pigtail hanging right down into a puddle. Two of the boys had started to pelt across towards the wire fence, and the hail of bricks followed them. It was a real rout.

Out of the corner of his eye again, Bernard saw a flashing movement at the same time as he heard a loud shout. He turned right, to see the Shofiq lad come roaring out of the garden of an old dumpy house like an express train. He'd dropped the wallbrick and picked up something that looked like a length of old rubber hose. It was about ten feet long, and grey, and an inch thick. What's more, he was swinging it round his head, round and round, faster and faster, as he ran.

Bernard was amazed. The lad was swaying with the weight of the hose whizzing round his head, sort of rocking as he ran. If it had gone much faster he would have taken off for sure, he looked so much like a helicopter. He shot towards Bobby Whitehead's lot at a terrific lick, yelling the top of his head off as he ran. The hail of rocks at the little kids stopped. They all got their wits back at once, even the girl that had been hit. They flashed across the croft bawling, a group of little frightened mice.

Bobby Whitehead shouted something, and Patsy Broome bent down to pick up a lump of iron at her feet. But it was too late, much too late. Bernard watched fascinated as the Pakistani lad got closer. The little'uns dropped their bricks and ran. Pat looked at Bobby and she'd gone white. He just stared, shocked, as the helicopter whirled towards him. He opened his mouth. Patsy pulled back her arm as if she was going to bung the lump of iron, then she dropped it. She started to back away. She looked terrified. The whooshing noise of the whirling hosepipe came clearly to Bernard's ears. The Pakistani lad's mouth was open, his face all twisted up. Big Patsy turned on her heels and ran.

It was obvious to Bernard that Bobby Whitehead was going to scarper too, it just had to happen. But he didn't get the chance. His gob was still wide open and he looked as if he'd wet himself. As he half turned, looking to where Pat was whistling over the croft towards the school, the helicopter arrived. As Bobby got his legs into action the hosepipe-end came whirling round, whooshing as it came. The tail-end of it caught him right across the side of the head, and he went down into a puddle with an icy splash.

Bernard, his own mouth wide open in admiration and horror, looked at the still form of the terrible Bobby Whitehead. His face was like a sheet and he wasn't moving. From under the hair above his ear a long curtain of blood started to flow.

The Pakistani lad had let go of the hosepipe and rubbed his hands on his jeans. He walked over to Bobby Whitehead's body and looked down at it. Then he looked towards the school and started to walk towards it. He was still panting, but that was all. Bernard skirted the fallen giant and scuttled in by a different gate. He felt quite peculiar; not at all like a secret agent.

14

# Chapter Two

IT was dead hard to concentrate in class, because the Pakistani lad sat not far away from Bernard, and he kept looking at him all the time; couldn't take his eyes off. The amazing thing was, he didn't seem worried, or feared, or the slightest bit upset. He just sat there, with his books, saying nothing as usual, although he must have known something was going to happen pretty soon, what with him killing Bobby Whitehead and that.

During assembly not a word had been said about it. Bernard had weighed up if he should tell one of the teachers, just in case they didn't know, but he thought in the end it was better to keep his mouth shut. Somehow or other teachers always *did* know, you could never tell them anything they hadn't heard of already, and in any case it was always better to keep out of things. He didn't particularly mind that this lad had murdered Bobby Whitehead – in fact on the whole he thought it was a good thing – but he didn't want to get himself mixed up in it. No one knew he'd seen, not the grown-ups, and that was the way he'd keep it.

In the few minutes after assembly and before Miss Todd came into the class he'd managed to gasp the news out to Maureen and Dougie though, so they kept rubber-necking at the lad as well. Terry, his other mate in the class, had had to go and clear up some rubbish he'd been seen chucking down in the playground, so he'd not heard. Maureen was quite comical about it. She'd gone all pale, and put her fingers in her mouth. She sat two desks away, and she'd sort of pulled herself right to the edge of her bench, as if she was putting as much room between them as she possibly could.

Sitting there over his books, Bernard couldn't help marvelling at it though. He wasn't big, wasn't this Shofiq lad, but he'd looked like a right terror. It was a real smart trick that swinging the hosepipe like a helicopter. Bobby Whitehead's face just before he turned to scarper off had been a sight for sore eyes. Bernard could see himself doing the same thing – he often bashed up Bobby Whitehead in his head – and he felt a surge of joy as the end of the hose smacked into his rotten earhole.

Miss Todd had been droning on about this, that and the other for what seemed ages when it happened. Bernard, along with everyone else in the overheated, damp-smelling classroom, lifted his eyes up gratefully when the door handle rattled. It was a funny, school-type door, with a wooden bottom and a frosted glass top. Even with the frosting you could tell who was outside, even if Bernard hadn't already guessed. Sure enough, the man who opened it, all big shoulders and bushy black hair, was Mr Ellis, the headmaster.

That was fair enough. But the person with him was a real shocker. It was Patsy Broome all right, still as ugly as a dancing pig with her frizzy hair sticking out all over the place, but she didn't half look different. Her jumper was pulled down neat and tidy, her skirt was straight, and her face was shiny and polished, as if she'd actually had a wash for once. He almost couldn't recognise her.

Bernard shut his mouth smartish and took a peek at the Shofiq lad. He was looking at Pat calmly, as if nothing had happened. Bernard wondered idly if Pakistanis went white when they were frightened. He reckoned he'd never know from this one. He was as cool as a cucumber.

Miss Todd looked up with her eyebrows raised in her 'Well, what is it this time?' expression. The headmaster gave her a nod, then said to Patsy: 'Well girl?' Then he smiled to the teacher and said: 'Excuse me for barging in, Miss Todd. I won't keep you a second.'

Pat Broome looked round the room with an expression on her face like some sort of angel. Pleased with herself, and good. Bernard felt himself blushing, although he knew he hadn't been seen. She's making a right good meal of it, he thought. Pretending she doesn't know who did it straight off. I ruddy wish she'd been killed as well, that's all.

In the end, when she'd done her act of studying every face in the class to make them feel like criminals, Pat Broome lifted her head up to Mr Ellis and mouthed something quiet. The headmaster bent his ear down and Patsy said it again, louder.

'That's him, sir,' she said, pointing at the Pakistani lad. 'He hit Bobby with a lead pipe, sir. He swung it round his head.'

There was a sudden jabbering from all the kids. 'I knew,' shouted Dougie proudly. 'I knew it were 'im!' Silly get, thought Bernard angrily. Can't tell him nothing, you can't.

Mr Ellis silenced them with a bellow. He had this frightening knack of going bright red, as if he'd been blown up. He could do it like a flash; anger seemed to shoot out of him; you could almost feel it cutting you. In the intense quiet Pat Broome said: 'Him there, sir. Him with the green jumper on.'

The headmaster stared at the Pakistani lad, and he stared back. Again Bernard marvelled. He didn't seem feared, not a bit. And he still hadn't gone white, no danger!

'Mm,' said Mr Ellis. 'Right, Patricia, off you go. Back to your class and quickly, girl.'

Pat Broome looked shocked.

'But, sir,' she started.

The red flooded back into the headmaster's cheeks. Before he had time to open his mouth she muttered, 'Yes, sir,' and bolted. When the door had closed Mr Ellis surveyed the children. Not a finger stirred.

'Miss Todd,' he said at last, 'what is that boy's name, if you please? Stand up, boy.'

'It is Rahman, Mr Ellis,' replied Miss Todd. 'Shofiq Rahman. Might I be permitted to know . . . ?'

The headmaster gave a weird smile, like a copper who's caught you bunging bricks or something.

'In brief, Miss Todd,' he said nastily, 'you appear to be harbouring a would-be assassin in your class. I will elaborate later.'

Bernard had no clear idea of what a would-be assassin was, but the effect it had on Miss Todd was alarming. She stuck out her hand and rested herself against her desk, with a funny noise in her throat. The headmaster laughed.

'I would like to see Mr Rahman in my office in five minutes if you please, Miss Todd. In the meantime you might care to ask him yourself what he is accused of. It might be illuminating for us to compare notes later.'

Still looking dazed, Miss Todd pushed herself upright.

'Yes, sir,' she said. 'Of course.'

'Good,' he said. 'In five minutes then.'

When he'd gone, pandemonium broke out. The Pakistani lad was still standing there and all the others in the class were shouting at him, and each other, to know what it was all about. The sight of Pat Broome looking like she'd been picking out Jack the Ripper – and when this lad had obviously done it – well crikey!

Dougie shouted: 'He belted Bobby Whitehead with a lump of . . .'

And then he broke off, because Bernard, in the confusion, had leaned across and punched him in the stomach as hard as he could without being seen.

'Shut your rotten mouth!' he said.

As the teacher got them calmed down, he sat in his desk panting. That fool Dougie. First he'd have told about the hosepipe, then about how his mate Bernard had seen

it all, then all hell would have gone off. He felt sick.
There was going to be trouble, big trouble. All he needed
was for Dougie to get *his* name mixed up in it. No rotten
thank you! He caught Maureen's eye. She still looked
afraid, but she gave him a little smile. *She* was all right,
she was a smasher. She'd probably keep Dougie's mouth
clamped, once she got the chance, because she was his
sister and belted him if he got out of line.

When everyone was quiet, Miss Todd put on her en-
couraging smile for the lad. He didn't smile back, although
he was looking at her full in the face. After a while she
went pinkish.

'Well, Shofiq,' she said. 'And what was all that about,
do you think?'

He opened up his hands in a funny, foreign way.

'I don't know, Miss,' he said.

There was a murmur from the class, instantly hushed.

'Oh come now, Shofiq,' Miss Todd went on. 'That won't
do, now will it! Patricia Broome comes in looking for
somebody quite definite, and says you attacked Robert
Whitehead with a lead pipe, and you know nothing about
it! Does that sound entirely likely?'

'I don't know, Miss,' said the lad quietly. 'But I'll have
to tell the headmaster something, so I'll leave it till then,
eh?'

Miss Todd went pinker yet. The Pakistani boy had a
funny way of talking to grown-ups; Bernard would never
have dared to go anywhere near it. He had a right strong
accent, too – not Pakistani, but Lancashire, just like the
rest of them, just like Bernard himself. Miss Todd was
getting angry, losing her rag, anyone could tell that.

'That is a very silly attitude to take, Shofiq Rahman,'
she snapped. 'It is apparent to me that you have been
fighting, and fighting with weapons. That is not a nice
thing, nor is it Br . . . allowed. You are going to get into
very serious trouble if you go on like this, and I wish to
know all about it. Now! Tell me exactly what happened!'

The whole class was entranced. It was absolutely smashing, to see Miss lose her rag over the way he was cheeking her. Then the Pakistani lad gave a kind of a shrug with his shoulders.

'I'd rather say nowt, Miss, if you don't mind,' he said, almost in a whisper. 'I'm quite willing to take what's coming from Mr Ellis.'

An odd feeling was coming over Bernard. He hadn't the faintest idea what this daft lad thought he was doing, but he knew it meant trouble. Miss Todd was a right bad-tempered old crow, and there was no doubt she was going to go up the wall in a minute or two, go really sky-high off her undercarriage. She thought he'd been doing a bit of private battering, and now he was being smart about it. Bernard didn't know why he just didn't speak out, say what Bobby Whitehead had been up to, but he wasn't going to, obviously. Kids all over the room were nudging each other in glee, making sure she didn't see them at it, because she'd turn on them then, no danger. It was a right pantomime, to see the Pakistani get himself in lumber.

'I will give you one more chance to be polite and sensible, Shofiq Rahman,' said Miss Todd icily. 'And then I wash my hands of the matter. Have you been indulging in violent fighting, or is there something else behind all this?'

Bernard could see that the eyes of the standing boy were very bright. To his amazement he felt tears prick his own eyes. He bit his lip. He was confused, dry-mouthed. He suddenly shot his hand up. Well, he didn't. It shot up of its own accord, there wasn't any way he could stop it.

'Please, Miss,' he said. 'It weren't him, Miss. It weren't his fault. It were the Whitehead lot. They were Paki . . . They were bunging . . . They were . . .'

The tension was electric. The Pakistani lad sat down, plonk, without being told. There was a low murmur of

20

voices, which faded away as Miss Todd waved her hand in the air.

'Oh?' she said, in a completely different tone of voice. 'What's this, Bernard? Robert Whitehead was what?'

In for a penny, in for a pound. Bernard gulped unhappily.

'He were Paki-bashing, Miss. Him and Pa . . . Him and some others. They were bunging bricks. That Sho . . . that lad there waded in to 'em and stopped 'em.'

Miss Todd was smiling.

'Well well,' she said. 'I never thought I'd live to see the day. Well well.'

Bernard sat there, bright red, feeling a proper duck-egg. The eyes of the other kids bored into him, in a shocked, almost horrified, way. Bernard Kershaw sticking up for a Paki? Never!

Miss Todd rapped abruptly on her desk lid.

'Right,' she said. 'Off you go then. Cut along and see Mr Ellis. And make sure you tell him the lot.'

The Pakistani lad got to his feet and walked towards the door. Miss Todd clicked her tongue.

'Come on, Bernard, come on! We haven't got all day to wait you know! Get along to Mr Ellis with Shofiq here!'

Bernard started to stutter. His heart sank into his soggy plimsolls. He blinked over and over again.

'Me, Miss? But, Miss, I . . . Please, Miss Todd, I mean . . .'

She smiled a big friendly smile.

'Now now, Bernard, don't be silly. Of course you must go along with Shofiq. You clearly have something to say of the greatest importance.'

'But, Miss. I don't know nothing about it. I mean I . . .'

She got all brisk again, her smile went frostier.

'No nonsense, Bernard, if you please. Just cut along with your friend now and speak to Mr Ellis quite firmly and clearly about what you saw. I have a feeling he will be exceedingly interested to hear it.'

Your friend! There was a titter from the kids around him. Bernard's face began to burn. The Pakistani boy was waiting by the door, not looking at anything, just standing, waiting. Miss Todd jerked her head sideways.

'Come! Get along with you now.'

Bernard went. When he reached the Pakistani lad they left the room together, walked along the disinfectanty corridors in silence. Oh my God, he thought: why didn't I keep my rotten mouth shut!

# Chapter Three

By the time they got to the headmaster's room, Bernard was practically dribbling with terror. He didn't get on particularly well with the teachers, although he found no trouble at all in being pretty good at his work: it was easy. Somehow or other he always said things the teachers didn't like, although he didn't usually do it on purpose. He'd once overheard a couple of them talking about him, that fat old barmpot Morrissey and a skinny, lanky student teacher girl they called Hairpin because she was so thin. 'Forward,' she'd said, in her funny Londony voice. 'That little Kershaw boy: very bright but inclined to be forward.' And old Morrissey, who he'd known for years and got many a clip from, said back: 'He's not forward, young lady, not what I'd call forward. I'd say he was a cheeky little get. If he gives you any trouble, kick his bottom. He won't mind.'

Morrissey was all right, but old Ellis was a different kettle of fish, no danger. He was big, and fierce, and inclined to go off into red rages. He was cruel too; it was well known he was almost sent to jail for ten years once for caning a little kid half to death. He'd only got off because the council had hushed it up. Now that this Pakistani lad had killed Whitehead and Bernard had given himself away on it, there'd be hell to pay. He had half an idea that if one of them went to jail the other one would go too. Something about seeing a murder done and not stopping it. It seemed unfair, but it happened all the time.

'I never seen nothing really,' he said once, hopefully, to the boy. 'I were miles away. Right over the croft.'

The Shofiq lad gave him a little smile. He had big eyes, huge, like a film star.

'Give over,' he said. 'You'll be all right, don't wet yourself.'

Standing outside the green-painted door, with 'Head-master – Knock and Wait' marked on it, Bernard felt as if he might do just that. His breakfast tea seemed to have decided to want to come out, all in a rush. He crossed his legs, uncomfortable and very miserable.

'Ee, heck,' he said. 'Let's beggar off.'

The Pakistani lad lifted up his fist and banged on the door as bold as brass. In the interval before the head-master replied he smiled again.

'You'll be champion,' he said. 'Give over worrying.'

The first thing that Bernard saw, when the order came and this Shofiq pushed the door open, was bad enough. Mr Ellis was standing behind his desk, not sitting, and he looked like a dirty great thundercloud. He was big, dead big, and horrible-looking, with monster shoulders like Frankenstein, and all this bushy black hair. Big black eyebrows, too, that stuck out far enough to put things on. His eyes, underneath them, glittered, in the second that Bernard managed to look at them.

As his own eyes, terrified, slid away from the head-master's face, he saw the second thing, and this time he nearly had a heart attack. Lying on the settee-thing, where all the sick kids ended up while Ellis decided whether to cane 'em for shamming or send 'em home, was Bobby Whitehead. He looked all funny and white, true enough, and he had a thick bandage wrapped round and round his nut. But dead he was not; not in the slightest. When Bernard had first glimpsed him he'd had a little smile on his face, satisfied and smug, expecting to see just the Paki lad he was going to get in lumber. But when he saw Bernard as well the smile went away. He

24

stared at him, puzzled. Then he put a pained expression on, as if he was fading away, desperately injured. The door closed behind them with a click.

'What are you doing here, Kershaw?' asked Mr Ellis. He sounded bad-tempered. Bernard swallowed.

'Please, sir, Miss Todd sent me, sir.'

'What for? Moral support? Prisoner and escort? Pilot fish and whale?'

Bernard blinked. Sometimes he wondered about the headmaster. People said he was mad. *Was* he mad?

'No, sir,' he said lamely. 'Yes, sir.'

'Good God, where do you people learn to speak English?' said the headmaster. 'Are you gibbering, boy? Are you an idiot? Yes, of course you are, of course you are, of course you are. I am beset by idiots, beset.'

He held on to his table with both hands, breathing hard. He only needs the bolt in his neck, Bernard thought, scared as he was. Frankenstein to the life. Mr Ellis went rapidly red, then slowly pink, then back to normal. He sat down with a great wheezy sigh.

'Stand up properly, both of you,' he said after a while. 'Shoulders back, stomachs in, chests out. Now, Rahman, kindly tell me why you apparently attempted to murder that boy there. You shut your mouth, Kershaw, or I'll cane you. And you, Whitehead. If you are to die of your wounds you'll probably live long enough to be thrashed before the undertaker arrives. Now speak.'

High on the wall behind the seated headmaster, on a pair of banged-in nails, there was a cane. The palms of Bernard's hands were sweating. The need to go to the lavvy was terrible. He was as miserable as sin. Bobby Whitehead, though, looked worse. He looked as if he was going to die on the spot. Bernard just hoped they had lavvies in prison, that was all.

The Pakistani lad's voice, when it came, shocked him. It was quiet, and polite, and firm. He didn't sound scared, he didn't sound worried, he didn't sound anything.

25

'I don't know what he's told you already, sir,' he said, nodding towards Whitehead, 'but this is what happened. My two little sisters, sir, that are in the infants, have been getting a bit of stick, sir. On their way to school, like. Two or three times last week, once the week before, lots of times before that, on and off.'

'Stick?' said Mr Ellis nastily. 'You mean the cane has been applied in the infants' school? That is a most unlikely allegation.'

There was a fairly long pause. The Pakistani lad didn't move. Out of the corner of his eye Bernard could see him looking at the headmaster. It was just typical of Ellis to take it wrong. He was a stickler for proper English. He reckoned the local folk didn't speak it, neither, the Cheshire get. Bernard suddenly hated him. Why couldn't he ruddy listen and stop being so clever? He seethed.

The Pakistani lad went on, as calm as ever.

'Sorry, sir. I mean, that on their way to school they've had a bit of trouble, sir. With some lads. With that lad Whitehead there. And his gang.'

Bobby Whitehead raised himself on one elbow with a screech of indignation.

'It's not true, sir! He's lying, the rotten ge . . . He attacked me, sir, he . . .'

Mr Ellis rose to his feet so fast that his table rocked. His face went brick red. His shout nearly blew Whitehead off the couch.

'Shut up!'

The noise ran round and round the room. Bernard's ears rang. He stared at the carpet. He wanted to cry. The Shofiq lad started to talk again, quiet and calm.

'My sister, the youngest one, sir, has got a cut face from last week. It upsets my mother, sir. She doesn't understand. Little friends too, sir. They usually come to school in a bunch, about a half dozen, sir. Today I followed them.'

Bernard stole a glance at Bobby Whitehead. He looked proper ill.

'So when you attacked Robert Whitehead, you did it to prevent an attack upon your sister?'

'After, sir. After an attack on my sisters. Two of them, sir.'

'Ah,' said Mr Ellis. 'So you do admit that you attacked this boy?'

Bernard got panicky. This daft Pakistani had given himself away. Now there'd be trouble. But Mr Ellis didn't sound like trouble, just for the second. He sounded down, like. Sort of depressed.

'Oh yes, sir. I found a piece of rubber hose and I hit him with it. I was a bit feared at first, in case I'd killed him, sir, but he seemed all right, lying in the puddle. Dead people don't bleed you know, sir. And he were bleeding right fast.'

Mr Ellis made a funny noise, a muffled snort. Bernard looked up sharpish, but he had his face hidden behind his hands. Was he crying?

After a few seconds Mr Ellis took his hands away. He said: 'You hit him very hard, you know. You *might* have killed him.'

'Aye,' said the Pakistani lad. 'I were right worried. But I had to make sure, like. I can't have it going on, sir. My mum gets feared, sir. She doesn't understand.'

There was a very long silence in the room. Bernard remembered that he'd wanted the lavatory, but the need had gone away. Bobby Whitehead looked terrible, white and tense, breathing fast.

'Well,' said Mr Ellis at last. 'This is all very interesting. Not at *all* what Mr Whitehead there says happened, absolutely and completely not at *all*. And of course, he has witnesses. Would you care to tell us again, Bobby? I'm sure Mr Rahman and Bernard here would be enchanted to hear your version of the facts. Come on, lad, on your feet, eh?'

27

Bobby Whitehead put on a great act, it was fantastic. He rolled his eyes, and looked like he was going to throw up. He sort of got halfway off the couch-thing, then dropped back. He opened up his mouth and stuck his tongue out, with a croaking noise.

'I can't, sir,' he said at last, all breathy and quiet. 'I don't think I can move, sir. I think he's broke me skull, sir.'

'It were only rubber, sir,' said Shofiq calmly. 'I hit him quite hard, but it were only a lump of rubber.'

Mr Ellis wiggled his eyebrows.

'According to this boy,' he said, 'it was a lump of lead. Are you sure it is not *you* who are swinging the lead, Robert Whitehead?'

'Sir?'

'Swinging the lead, boy, means avoiding something by pretending to be ill, or hurt, or otherwise indisposed. I want you on your feet, boy, and I want it now. Stand!'

Bernard was fascinated. He'd often got off school by kidding on his mum that he wasn't feeling too good – one day he'd mixed up some spit with some pearl barley he used for his peashooter, to make it look like sick on the bedroom floor – but he'd never done it as well as Whitehead did. When he finally made it to his feet he was rocking, like he'd been knocking back the beer dregs at Christmas. He was ill-looking all right, no danger. But he must be putting it on, if Mr Ellis said so.

'Good,' said the headmaster. 'Now, boy, tell us again what you say happened.'

Bernard could guess Bobby Whitehead's problem. He didn't know what he, Bernard, was doing there. He'd obviously thought no one had seen what happened, except for him and Patsy Broome. He'd obviously cracked on this Pakistani lad had belted him up just for the fun of it. It was a laugh really. Bernard was enjoying it, to his surprise. He gave Whitehead a sudden leer, a rude, nasty smirk, when Mr Ellis wasn't looking.

At last Whitehead spoke. His voice was trembly, and he kept up his swaying.

'It weren't us that bunged – threw – the stones, sir,' he said. 'Me and Patsy tried to stop 'em. It were some little-'uns, sir. Honest.'

Mr Ellis smiled.

'Name them,' he said.

Whitehead didn't bat an eyelid.

'Georgie Greenwood, sir, in 1x. Bertie Smith, sir, him that's in the same class. And Freddie Wright. Him too. 1x.'

'And you and Patricia Broome tried to stop them?'

Bobby Whitehead had stopped swaying. His colour was better. He thought he was getting away with it.

'Yes, sir,' he said. 'I mean, that Pak . . . that lad there might of *thought* it were us, like, but he couldn't see. He were too far away. We had rocks in our *hands*, like, but only to frighten off the little'uns; them that was doing the chucking, sir. Then he come at us, sir. Like a nutter, sir. And tried to kill me.'

Half expecting him to deny it hotly, Bernard turned to the boy beside him. Shofiq Rahman's big brown eyes merely stared gently at Bobby Whitehead.

'Well?' said Mr Ellis. 'What do you say to that, Mr Rahman?'

'He's a liar, sir,' said the Pakistani lad. 'Ask this boy, sir. I think he must have seen it, sir.'

All their eyes turned to Bernard. The clear brown ones, Mr Ellis's that he couldn't meet, and Bobby Whitehead's. It was Bobby Whitehead's that he didn't like most. They were cold, and unwavering, and speaking straight across the room. What they said was very clear: 'Open your mouth, Bernard Kershaw, and you're a dead man.'

'Ah,' said Mr Ellis. 'So that is why you are here, Kershaw. You saw it all. You were at the scene of the crime. Tell me, Kershaw,' he went on, 'why are you always at the scene of the crime? Why are you always to be found where there is trouble?'

That wasn't fair. But it worked. Bernard, who had decided to deny everything and leave this Pakistani to his fate, blurted out: 'It weren't me, sir! Nothing to do with it! I just happened to be watching, sir, that's all. I never even buzzed a brick!'

What happened next was amazing, and shocking, and a good laugh, when you thought about it. Bobby Whitehead, who'd gone dead white again, threw up all over the carpet. He hadn't been shamming after all. He got sent to hospital later, but they sent him home in the afternoon, to rest up a bit.

It pleased Bernard, for a while, that he'd actually been hurt, even if he wasn't going to die. It also pleased him when he thought of the trouble he'd get in, when he was fit enough, for stoning the little curry kids. It took some time for it to sink in that he, Bernard Kershaw, had got Bobby Whitehead in this lumber. Then he got really scared. That lad was a terror, and he had a gang. The Luger under his armpit suddenly became worthless. When Bobby Whitehead got round to it, he was in for a battering. And who was going to get *him* out of the mire?

# Chapter Four

THE obvious person, of course, although it didn't occur to Bernard as such, was Shofiq Rahman. During the dinner break he didn't see him, or anyone else, and he didn't think much about what was going on. After his school dinner he had to run home to do some chores, and to pick up a prescription for his mum. She was inclined to be pale and wan and quiet these days, since the do with the baby, and Bernard often had to waste valuable time doing things he reckoned weren't up to him. He'd given her a cup of tea and a sandwich, and she'd smiled and chatted to him a bit, which was nice, although she didn't show any interest in his problems. On his way back to school he'd got caught in a sleet storm and become an Arctic trawler battling through the pack-ice for a while, which had driven all his fearful thoughts away.

In the classroom Miss Todd had stuck him next to the radiator and dried his hair on a towel, as if he was someone special. Then she went into quite a long drone about how Bobby Whitehead and a couple of others had been caught doing something very disgusting and awful, and how someone had been very brave and honest and done the right thing. At first, when he'd worked out that she meant him, Bernard had been very embarrassed. He'd gone all red, and stared at the floor. At one point she'd actually asked him to come out in front of the class and tell them about it, but he'd just nearly died, and tried to hide under his desk.

A few of the lads had had a giggle at him, till they realised that Miss Todd was dead serious, and even good old Maureen had eyed him up a shade funny, like. The Pakistani lad, Shofiq, who it was meant to be about as well, sat there in his usual way, never saying a dickie-bird. In fact most of the time he was scratching away at the top of his desk-lid with a good little knife with a sort of pearly handle.

A lot of teachers went on about the Pakis and the blackies a lot of the time, till it was dead boring. The way they went on you were meant to think they were dead smashing, or interesting, or different or something, instead of just being kids with daft clothes and a funny pong to them, them that ate curry all the time. Now here was Miss Todd, who was usually a right snotty old bird, all skinny and a pointed nose, going on as if Bernard and this lad were heroes, or big mates.

'If there was a little more of this getting together, children,' she said, 'think what a nicer place school would be altogether. People like Robert Whitehead should always be reported, but if more of you would take a leaf out of Bernard's book, and do something *positive*, there would be no such problem. If anyone is the victim of bullying, and anyone else sees it, the thing to do is to help, instantly and without fear. Help each other, all of you, and school will be a nicer place.'

Bernard's mate Terry, who was good at English and always asking daft questions, poked his hand up.

'Please, Miss,' he said. 'What's positive? What does it mean, do something *positive*?

'I thought,' he added smugly, just to show how much he knew about everything, 'I thought it was the opposite of negative, like in a battery, you know.'

Bernard didn't listen to Miss Todd's reply. He was looking at his desk-lid, and his mood was changing fast. He wasn't embarrassed any more (anyway, Terry would probably keep the old crow going for ages, he could really twist her round his finger with his dopey questions) and he had got the beginning of an idea. He sneaked a glance at the Pakistani lad, who was still scratching away with his knife. It had occurred to him that he was a tough little ombree, and it had occurred to him that he owed Bernard a favour. In fact the more he thought about it, the more convinced he became. He'd practically saved this lad's life, when it came down to it, because until Bernard had spoke up, it had been more or less a hanging matter. Bobby Whitehead would have swore black was blue that he'd belted him with a lump of lead, and that ugly Pat Broome would have backed him up. This Shofiq would have gone to jail, or the juvenile court, or whatever, and that would have been that. And every morning, from that day on, Whitehead's lot would have belted up the Paki kids to their hearts' content.

Since his mate Mickie had got himself squashed on the railway, Bernard had been at a loose end, to be quite honest. He had the gang, fair enough. But what did it all add up to, when all was said? There was Terry, who was smart enough, and didn't get cold feet if they had the odd brush with the Glossop Street lot, and didn't always go whining home to his mum if he fell off a wall and cut himself. He was all right, but he was a nuisance too, in some ways. His brother was in the Air Force cadets, and played in the band on Sunday mornings, and Terry was always going off and hanging around him, in case he got a go at banging the big drum, or helping fly the model planes and that. You couldn't depend on Terry.

Then there was Maureen and Dougie McIlroy. Now Maureen was all right, she was smashing. He'd been in love with Maureen, and they'd done kissing and all that sort of stuff; but since they'd got over it, mostly, she'd been even better. She could fight any lad of her own age and she didn't scratch or bite, neither. She'd socked him once, when he'd said her baby brother looked like a monkey, and she'd made his nose bleed. She wasn't bad.

Dougie though. He was a different matter. He was big, and a bit slow, and a cry-baby. He'd tag along, and do all the things Bernard told him to, but he just wasn't any fun. If they were in the buildings, say, and a grown-up shouted at them, or a cop car went past ten streets away, he'd quite likely burst into tears, or hide, or scarper off home sharpish. Maureen bashed him about some, but even that was no satisfaction, because she wouldn't let anyone else have a go. He was right at the bottom of the class, and Bernard thought on the sly that he was a trifle on the backward side. All in all, he was a bit of a pain.

As a gang, let's face it, it was a dead loss. He pondered on Mickie. Mickie had been his mate, his real, blood-brother, share everything, fight to the death together mate. They *were* blood-brothers in fact, because Terry had read about it in some book, where these kids had cut their fingers and rubbed in the blood and swore to stand by each other. When it came to it, only him and Mickie had cut themselves, which was something like what happened in the book too, but he'd been glad. They'd done it on their own, in the ruined engine-shed behind the Daisy Mill, and Mick had stuck the knife in too far and bled like a stuck pig and had to go to hospital in case he needed stitches. They'd just told him off, actually, and wrapped it in a gauze bandage that the gang later used for playing pirates with.

It still made him feel sick, when he thought of the day Mickie had got killed. He hadn't been with him, which made it worse. And he hadn't been with him because he was chicken, which made it worse still. They'd been playing on the railway a lot, and Mickie had got more and more mad, darting out in front of the trains just before they came out of the tunnel with their horns going. When Bernard's dad had found out he'd been doing it he'd belted him so hard he hadn't been able to walk, hardly, for a week. He'd told him if he ever did it again he'd kill him, which would have been pointless when you thought about it, seeing as how he was trying to stop him getting killed by a train – but he meant it, or something pretty close.

The thing was, Bernard had been glad. Not of the beating, because that was like nothing he'd ever had, before or since. He was glad because he'd been given his excuse. All the other things he'd been warned not to do, that he'd promised blue was green he'd never do again, he did, anytime he felt like it. But he wouldn't go on the tracks again, not for anything. Because he was chicken.

Mickie had got beat too. Bernard's dad had told Mickie's dad and Mickie's dad had whipped him with an elastic thing off his roof-rack, with a hook on it. Two weeks after that, on a Sunday it was, Mickie had got killed. He'd gone off without Bernard, they'd had a row, and Bernard had cried in the Daisy engine-shed. And they'd picked up bits of Mickie in a bucket, spread from Ratcliffe to Victoria he was.

Bernard was jerked back to the present by Miss Todd repeating his name.

'Bernard,' she said, sharply. 'Have you been listening? I said you can help your friend Shofiq hand out the Scripture books and collect in the pencils.'

'Yes, Miss, sorry Miss,' he said, looking all bright and interested. This was her soft way of giving you a treat, letting you hand out books. He caught Maureen's eye, and he winked. But she was looking at him in a funny way. He realised what Miss had said. 'Your friend Shofiq.'

As they put out the books, he and the Pakistani lad passed close to each other. Bernard took a crafty sniff. Sure enough, there was the curry shop smell. They were a funny lot, no danger, and obviously they didn't go in for washing much. But then, to be fair – and he was only being fair because his mind was already half made up – to be fair he, Bernard, didn't wash much either. Even if *he* didn't smell.

This lad, this Pakistani lad, owed him plenty. He'd

saved his life. You'd think he'd show it somehow, show his gratitude. As they passed again, Bernard looked him full in the face and smiled. It was a daft smile, a false smile. It felt uncomfortable on his mouth. The big brown eyes looked into his.

'Hiya,' said Bernard lamely.

' 'Ello, lad,' replied Shofiq Rahman. 'Thanks.'

He'd said it! Bernard went back to his table blushing furiously. He was trembling inside. That Paki lad had said thanks! As he sat there staring blankly at his page of Scripture, all sorts of ideas formed in his head. New ideas, great ideas. If he let him join the gang, they could do all sorts of things. He vividly remembered the flailing helicopter, it had been great. And although he never said much, Bernard knew he was not a dummy. He was good at all his subjects, better than most of the kids, better than Bernard at some things, and he made ace models in handicrafts, really smart things.

Over the next hour or two he dreamed happily of dangerous deeds undertaken, fantastic exploits achieved. Some of the things he'd done with Mickie, like hunting for gold, or climbing up the inside of the Raven Mill chimney when they'd broken open the boilershed during Wakes, some of the things that the gang ought to do but somehow he could never get them round to it any more. Most of all he dreamed about routing Bobby Whitehead and that crow Patsy Broome. Let alone them filling him in for telling on them over the business that morning, he'd be able to chase them from hell to breakfastime, as his dad would say. He'd get a lump of hosepipe too, and they could both be helicopters. They'd put the fear of Jiminy up them; that Whitehead would never be the same lad.

Problem was, how was he going to get hold of this Shofiq and sort it all out? In the muck-up at the end of the afternoon he might just lose him. Miss Todd had this potty way of sending them all out in batches, so she never had the trouble some of the teachers had over noise, and thundering hordes of kids all pelting down the corridors at once. And you never knew which batch you were going to be in. That was crafty too – it meant if someone was planning to batter someone they never knew if they'd get the chance – and old Toddy seemed to have a good idea on who wanted to bash who, as well. All in all, she was a rotten nuisance was Miss Todd, a real strictie.

In the end, he decided to send a note. Although they were meant to be doing quiet reading at this point, he had no trouble getting a bit of paper hidden down beside his book and a little stub of pencil out of his pocket. He sucked it for a minute or two, waiting for inspiration, then decided on the dead straight approach.

'Dear Shoffeek.' Point one: he didn't know how to spell his rotten name! He guessed that was near enough though.

'If Miss sends you out before me could you hang about so I can see you urgent, it is imperrative I see you. If she sends me out before you I will do same. Do not speak to anyone about this it is imperrative secresy is maintained.'

That was that, almost. But it was the almost that was the hard part. How should he sign it?

Bernard pondered for a long time, not forgetting to flick over the page of his book every now and then; Bernard the Black Hand was a highly-trained spy, a match for any old teacher, even Miss Cat's Eyes Todd. His mind drifted back to the morning – the flailing hosepipe, the hail of bricks, the screaming kids, the beautiful sight of Shofiq Rahman laying low the terrible Bobby Whitehead. He made up his mind.

He sucked the pencil and wrote heavily: 'Signed: Your friend Bernard Kershaw.'

That gave him a little tremor to write, so he wrapped up the paper quickly, before he could change his mind. He wrote 'Shoffeek (the Paki)' on it and passed it along the line. There was one very bad moment. When it got to Maureen and she read the address she almost choked.

She looked at Bernard in a funny way, an annoyed way. Then she started to unfold the paper.

For no real reason that he could pin down, Bernard felt panic rising in his chest. He signalled frantically to Maureen not to read the letter, but she carried on unfolding it. He half rose from his seat, knocking his books onto the floor with a clatter.

'Bernard,' said Miss Todd irritably. 'What are you up to, boy? Sit down at once and get on with your reading. What page are you up to?'

By the time he'd got himself sorted out and Miss Todd calmed down, the letter had been read, refolded, and passed on. He glared at Maureen angrily, and she glared back. Something was wrong, no doubt of that. He thought he knew what, as well. He stuck his tongue out, and got shouted at in a very angry way by Miss Todd.

The Pakistani boy glanced at Bernard when he'd read the note, but he didn't smile or anything. He folded it up and stuffed it into his right-hand jeans pocket. Bernard hoped he'd write a reply, but of course it was not needed, and anyway he might not have a pencil handy. He went back to his book and read a few lines. Then he gave up, and made up what he'd say to the lad after school.

It never happened. Shofiq left in the first batch, along with Maureen and Terry and a few others. Bernard got out last, after collecting up all the books because he'd stuck his tongue out. Maureen, Terry and Dougie were waiting all right, but the Pakistani lad had vanished.

'He went straight off,' said Maureen complacently. 'He never even waited a second.'

'Like a rocket,' said Terry. 'The Brown Streak!'

'Anyway,' said Maureen, dangerously. 'What's all this "Your friend Bernard Kershaw", eh? You turned soft then? If you ask me ...'

'Get lost, you,' Bernard snarled. He started to move off, fast, although he guessed the others would be wanting to talk about the fight and all.

'Hey!' shouted Maureen. 'What's up, Bern? Hey, come back. Dougie's got some money for sweets. Hey!'

Bernard did not look round. He put his head down and pelted for Middleton Road as fast as he could. He was pig sick.

# Chapter Five

IT was dinnertime the next day before Bernard got to talk to any of them again, and he still hadn't had a word or a glance off the Pakistani lad. On his way to school he'd been Bernard the Black Hand with a vengeance, because he had more than half an idea that Bobby Whitehead and Co would be lying in wait. In fact, so sure was he that he would be set on and done up if he wasn't dead sharp, that he even broke his golden rule and went across the lollipop. It made him uncomfortable, it made him think of Mickie again; the main reason he never usually used the lollipop man was because of Mickie. He'd let him down by being chicken once, and he hated to admit it. Crossing Middleton Road in all the early traffic, and especially the big lorries coming down the hills from Yorkshire, was proof enough. No chicken would take the daft risks he took, just to cross the road.

Once he was across he'd gone right into the spy routine. He'd skirted round the croft dead slow, eyeing up everyone that passed. He'd lurked for ages in the doorway of the Musicians, too, because he knew that Whitehead lived off Spring Lane, that ran down to it. But he hadn't even seen him. Not him, nor Big Patsy Broome.

He hadn't caught a glimpse during assembly, either. It was one of those annoying things. When you weren't looking out for someone, or thinking about them, you were always seeing them, or bumping into them. But today, when he glanced around the hall so often that he had his ear clipped by Mr Saxby in the end, he didn't see anyone. Maybe Bobby Whitehead had never come back, he mused. Maybe it had been more serious than old Ellis reckoned, and he'd died in the night. But that was not likely, he guessed. All the teachers were there as usual, bored and boring, yawning and rubbing their eyes during the boring old prayers.

On his way into class he'd caught a sight of the Pakistani lad's green jumper up in front and sped up to catch him. He didn't plan on saying anything, like; just wanted to be near him to see if he smiled, or nodded, or said Hiya. As he jumped out of the line he knocked over a little girl going down to the babies though, and another teacher, a woman, clouted his ear. He'd end up like a boxer one day, he reckoned, all the beltings his earholes got.

Bernard didn't have to run any errands after his dinner today, so he and Terry, and Maureen and Dougie, ended up in their special warm spot behind the boiler room, out of the wind. It was so cold that most of the kids stayed in the hall, screaming and shouting, as if it was a real treat to be allowed to keep in. But cold or no cold, Bernard and his lot weren't having any of that.

They talked about general things, about this and that, to start with, after they'd finished flicking all the baked beans over the wall that Dougie had saved from his dinner.

'It's ruddy daft, I call it,' said Terry. 'All them little twerps staying in in their dinnertime. They ought to get out and get some fresh air. It's good for you, fresh air is.' He breathed in noisily, his chest swelling till the zip on his anorak bulged.

Dougie went into an old man that smokes too much routine. He filled his lungs, and coughed and rolled about and spat. It was quite funny for a while, till he kept it up too long as usual.

'Give over, our Dougie,' said Maureen after a few

41

minutes. 'You're a right fool, you are, the way you go on.'

Dougie was hurt, so he started all over again, until Maureen twisted his arm. He stopped, looking grumpy for a few seconds. Then he forgot it and started to pick his nose.

Bernard wiped his nose on his sleeve. It was dripping all the time.

'It's right brass monkey weather,' he said. 'I don't know how that Pakistani lad lives, him with only a jersey on and all.'

He made his voice casual, but nobody was kidded one scrap. There was a pause, an uncomfortable pause. Maureen and Terry looked at each other, but it was up to Maureen to speak, she was the boss, after Bern.

Before she said anything, Maureen started to kick at a loose brick in the boiler room wall. She had on a pair of pink plastic shoes, with a crossover strap. Above these, and her white socks, her legs were all scratched, and pale from the cold, with goose pimples. She had a blue dress on, that the wind gusting round the corner flattened round her thighs, till her yellow anorak, tight at her waist, kept it in round her bottom. She kicked for quite a time, with Bernard studying her. He wondered what she'd say. She'd been dead browned off with him yesterday, what his dad called miffed. Her blonde hair covered up most of her face. He was half feared of her.

'Well you should know then, Bernard Kershaw,' she said. 'He's your mate, isn't he?'

'What you on about, you fool,' he said. 'I don't hardly know the lad. I just wondered, that's all.'

'Oh, get him!' said Maureen to the wall, as if it was a person she was having a chat to. ' "I just wondered, that's all"! Oh, get him!'

Dougie sniggered, but not for any reason. He was blinking, a sure sign he didn't know what was going on properly.

'Ah, shut up,' said Bernard crossly. 'Stupid woman.'

'Seriously though,' Terry said, in his 'seriously though' way. 'You did write him a note, Bernard, didn't you?'

'Saved his life,' said Dougie stoutly. 'That Bobby White-head would of killed him, eh?'

'Yeah,' said Bernard sourly. 'I wrote *him* a note. Not *her*, old Nosey Parker there.'

The wind whistled coldly round the shed. They weren't getting anywhere. It was a right old waste of time. Maureen went on kicking. Then she tossed her head, clearing the short thick hair off of her forehead. She smiled, a warm, nice smile. Bernard still thought she was dead pretty sometimes, it caught him unawares. He wouldn't have minded being on kissing terms just then, it would've been nice. She had big light-blue eyes and fair eyebrows. She laughed.

'Oh come on, Bernard,' she said. 'You don't mind me reading your daft old letter, do you? I don't mind you reading mine.'

'Yeah,' he said shortly. 'Only 'cause you never write none, that's all.'

'I'll write you one this afternoon if you like. What shall I say? From the Queen of Sheba? She was a blackie too, you know!'

They all laughed. But it was out, it had been said. With the ice broken they all started to chuck questions at him. Bernard couldn't keep up with the answers, but it didn't matter. What they wanted to do was to tell him what they thought, to show him how weird he was being, not to hear *why*. Did he know what Pakis ate? Did he know they never washed? Did he know the Government was going to send 'em all back to India with a hundred pounds to buy themselves a farm? The stories started flowing thick and fast.

It was Terry who knew most. Terry's dad, like Bernard's, worked in a cotton mill, but the one he was at was far bigger than most. Millions and millions of spindles, probably the biggest mill in the whole district. They had thousands of blokes working for them, and a good number of them were Pakistanis. As at Bernard's dad's mill, they mostly worked the nightshift.

'They have to work at night, see, so that the people don't see 'em all over the town in the day,' said Terry. 'If you have all these Pakistanis around all during the day, it puts up the rates or something. People don't like it, they start to talk, so they all work nights, like. They all turn up in droves, about six or seven o'clock of an evening, in mini-buses, you must have seen them.'

They all had, of course. Quiet, thin men mostly, with short coats on and packets of sandwiches or something in their hands. Terry got on to their food in a minute or so.

'My dad says they eats stuff that's right disgusting,' he said. 'Real trash. A tramp wouldn't touch it, not a proper English one.'

'No,' said Maureen. 'That can't be right. Some of the little kids here has school dinners, don't they?'

Terry was scornful.

'Oh yeah, *some*,' he said. 'But how many, eh? About one or two, that's all. And how many *are* there, eh? Dozens! Hundreds! Well, dozens anyway.'

Dougie said: 'What sort of food though, Terry? I mean, why's it disgusting?'

Terry put on a really horrified face.

'You won't believe this,' he said. 'But it's no word of a lie, my dad would swear it on the Bible he would. They eats green rice pudding. It's true! *Green!* Rice pudding! All the time, never nothing else! *Green!'*

They shuddered. Bernard, who'd been inclined to argue, suddenly remembered the warm, scenty smell coming off the lad the day before. Green rice pudding. Yuck!

Terry saw that he had them captured.

'And cat meat!' he said. 'Everyone knows that. That café in the middle of town, near the Health Centre. It were raided by the police. Cat meat!'

44

Maureen's voice was small and breathy.

'What did they find, Terry?' she asked. 'What, Kitty-cat, that sort of stuff? In the curry?'

'Nah!' said Terry. 'Worse. *Cats. Real* cats. Dead, hanging up in the fridge. They'd been catching them all over town. There was a scandal, it were in all the papers. They was making people eat *cats*.'

Dougie's eyes were round.

'Coo,' he gasped. 'I never did like Pakis, me! Coo!'

'Our cat disappeared,' Maureen said, in wonder. 'Ee, crikey, our Dougie! What if . . . Crikey, I bet it got ate. Crikey!'

Bernard wiped the drips off the end of his nose and said nothing. He knew a couple of stories about the Pakistanis too, but he was dead certain he wasn't going to tell them. How the night shift at his dad's mill went to the lavvies all the time to have a pray, and never did no work. One day his dad said some fellows had chucked a bucket of water over the top of the lavvy door, where this old fellow had been kneeling on a mat, praying. You should have heard him yell, his dad had said: it were a right giggle! He called the whirling helicopter to mind, the laying low of Bobby Whitehead. He noticed that Maureen was staring at him.

'I never thought you'd be mates with a smelly blackie, anyway,' she said. 'And you aren't half going to cop it when Bobby Whitehead catches up with you. You didn't half get him into trouble.'

'Oh dry up, you daft pig,' he said sullenly. 'I can see old Whitehead off any day. Don't you worry about me, that's all.'

'Anyway,' said Maureen. 'His mum's potty, did you know that? That Shofiq lad. He's got a potty mum. She's been in St James's.'

'Yeah,' said Dougie. 'I heard that. His mum's a loonie. His sister's potty too, she gets bussed to our mum's school.'

Over the other side of the playground the buzzer was going for the end of dinnertime. One of the teachers blew a whistle, loud and long. Bernard felt awful. Ruddy hell, he'd only spoke up for this lad, said a couple of words that's all. Anyone'd think he'd robbed a bank, the way everyone was going on.

'My mum's a dinner lady at Glossop Street,' said Maureen, as if everyone didn't know. 'That lad's sister keeps playing truant 'cause she has to get bussed. And his mum's a loonie. It's true.'

Terry nodded his head wisely.

'You'd better steer clear it seems to me, Bernard,' he said gloomily. 'I reckon you could get yourself in a lot of trouble there.'

Bernard, suddenly fed up, said something very short and rude and ran round the boiler room without them. As he came up to the door, Patsy Broome stepped out from behind the corner wall. He jumped. He didn't try to get past though; there wasn't a lot of point trying to avoid Pat, if she didn't want to be avoided. She was built like a tank, only twice as ugly, all teeth and fuzzy hair and as fat as a pig. She gave him a nasty smirky smile.

' 'Lo then, teacher's pet,' she said. 'Hurrying in to give Miss an apple, are you?'

'Aw dry up, you,' said Bernard. 'I'm fed up with all you lot. You just leave me be, that's all.'

Other kids were pushing past them to get to their classes. Pat's face was all white and chapped with cold. She must have been waiting for him.

'Just listen, you,' she said, glaring at him. 'Bobby Whitehead wants a *word* with you after school. Do you get me? He wants to have a *chat*, like. Do you know what I mean? He wants to *talk*.'

'I'm not scared of no Bobby Whitehead,' said Bernard defiantly. 'You tell him from me . . .'

Pat Broome stuck out a big hand and grabbed the front of his anorak. She was only the same age as him, but she

46

shook him about with no effort.

'Just shut your manky little mouth and listen,' she said. 'Bobby ain't been in today, but he's coming after school. He wants to see you in the Muscovy. You be there, right? He wants a *word*.'

Maureen and Terry and Dougie went past, on their way in. They glanced at him coldly; they didn't smile. They pretended they didn't know him. Pat shook him again.

'After school,' she repeated. 'You be there, Bernie Kershaw. You be there.'

# Chapter Six

BERNARD knew jolly well what Bobby Whitehead meant by 'having a talk'. He walked to his classroom dry-mouthed and sat at his desk in a daze. His hand automatically reached under his left armpit to pat the Luger, but he didn't actually notice himself doing it. He managed to listen to Miss Todd long enough to get what lesson it was, and he got out his book and opened it up to the right place. But he was worried. He was sick.

He looked out of the high old windows of the classroom at the thick grey clouds blowing fast across the sky. The weather was cold and rotten – it had been a rotten winter all along so far – but somehow he felt colder than he ought to. It was hot enough inside the school; hot and smelly, with damp clothes drying, and chalk, and that funny pong from lots and lots of rotten kids that never changed their socks. He was unhappy, dead depressed, and all because of something that didn't seem to add up to nothing. He'd fallen out with Maureen and that lot, and this Pakistani lad didn't want to know, and now Bobby and Pat were going to belt him up in the Muscovy. It wasn't fair, there just wasn't no justice in it at all. He looked at Maureen, head down, tongue caught between her lips as she concentrated. She wasn't pretty after all, she was an ugly little slutchpump. And her rotten blouse was dirty. When it started raining, a heavy, sleety rain, that ran down the window panes like grey paint, almost turning to ice, it made him feel better. *He* felt cold and awful, and outside it was too. That was how it should be.

As it happened, it was the weather that gave him a ray of hope. All through the first couple of lessons it banged away at the windows. For a time it turned to snow, piling up whitely at the base of the sills, and even when it went back to water again it was oozy, liquid ice. When the buzzer went for break Miss Todd said there was no question of them going out, none at all. All those for the toilets were to go in files of two or three, anyone who dawdled would be for it, and no water play or it would be a visit to Mr Ellis and no messing.

Bernard didn't want to go to the lav, couldn't even be bothered to go out for the sake of a wander. He sat in his desk thinking of being thumped, and wishing he was at home in bed, in his submarine. Maybe he could pretend to be took ill, that would do the trick. But he'd never fool Miss Todd, old Cat's Eyes. She was a right old crow.

Playtime was almost over, although he'd never even moved, when he realised someone was standing beside him, as if they wanted to say something. He thought it was Maureen, trying to make it up, so he kept his eyes glued to the desk-lid. Funnily enough, carved in it, with the front of his compass, were the words 'I love Moreen', done last year, before he'd even known how to spell her name. He sniffed. Love her my foot! Hate her, more like.

'Hey listen, pal,' said the figure, and he looked up in shock. It was the Pakistani lad, that Shofiq. There was half a smile on his mug, and a bit of his dinner, stuck on his chin.

'Oh!' said Bernard. He blushed. 'Oh, hello lad.'

'Listen, pal,' Shofiq repeated. 'I got your note all right but I had to go off, you know. Did you get on all right? I mean, I would've met you, but, you know.'

'Yeah,' said Bernard. 'What d'yer mean, "get on"? I mean, yeah, I saw you'd got my note.'

'Aye, well,' said the lad. He looked shy. 'Well look,' he said. 'I heard that Whitehead was going to batter you,

49

like. I mean, I were going to hang on, like. Just in case.'

Bernard was filled with a great hot feeling. Real happiness ran into his stomach. He grinned, however hard he tried not to.

'Hey!' he said. He managed to wipe the grin off, but it was an effort. 'Oh,' he went on. 'That's all right. No bother. I mean . . . Bobby Whitehead, well what's he, anyway?'

Shofiq nodded his head, seriously.

'Aye,' he said. 'You're right, I reckon. He's nowt. All right then. See you.'

As he turned away, Bernard let out a squeak. It sounded ruddy daft, he knew that. He was crimson as the Pakistani lad looked at him again. Neither of them spoke. Then he said: 'You've got a bit of mince on your chin. You know. Well, curry I spose.'

He blushed even harder. The lad felt about with his dark brown fingers till he found it. He picked it off his face, looked at it, then flicked it onto the floor. Miss Todd banged her desk-lid. Playtime was over.

'Thanks,' he said.

Bernard gabbled it out: 'Look, pal, do us a favour will you? I mean, after school tonight. That big fat cow Patsy Broome and Whitehead. They're going to do me over. I mean both of 'em; the whole gang. D'you reckon . . .?'

Miss Todd said loudly: 'Bernard. Shofiq. Sit down and stop talking please. Breaktime is over. This instant.'

The Pakistani lad gave a small grin as he turned to go.

'One good turn, eh? I'll see you after. By the side gate.'

'Shofiq Rahman! Get to your table this instant! And you, Kershaw: you can read to us all from page 140 of your green story book!'

Reading aloud was no trouble to Bernard. He did it so easily he even sometimes said 'were' where the book said 'was', which was the way people spoke mostly in their town but the teachers reckoned was worse than murdering someone. This day he sailed through it; he'd done three pages in a flash and would've gone on all afternoon if he'd been allowed. He wasn't taking it in, like, just letting the words spill out. He didn't even notice, at first, when Miss Todd told him to stop.

The next reader was a right stumbler, about half a word an hour, and he got to thinking about the coming fight. He patted his Luger firmly now, cleaned it and oiled it in his mind. He had Bobby Whitehead and Pat Broome lined up against the wall in the old smelly mill. The pistol in his right hand wavered. He weighed up whether to let them have it clean, straight between the eyes, or in the stomach, so they'd writhe in agony for an hour or two before they died.

There was a heavy flurry of hail against the window for a few minutes, then the sky cleared over the next half hour. By the time the final buzzer went, it was quite fine out. Cold, windy, and fine. Bernard felt a twinge of panic. Even with the Pakistani lad . . . well. He just hoped he had a lump of something handy today. Pity he wasn't allowed to carry his hosepipe, like a cowboy's lassoo.

Bernard might have got away with it, all things considered, but as it was, everything went wrong; everything. For a start-off, he was sent out in the first batch. That Miss Todd being fair as usual; she had no brains at all. Because he'd been kept late yesterday, Bernard was one of the first to go today. It was just typical – the worst possible thing that could happen.

He hung around in the cloakroom as long as possible, but that wasn't long. They had a system in his school, and it worked. After he'd fiddled about with his anorak for about twenty seconds flat, the duty teacher came up.

'Anything wrong? What are you waiting for?'

Bernard woggled his zip, as if it might be stuck. But it was a waste of time. He mumbled something into the fur collar and stomped out.

There weren't many kids hanging around, it was so

cold. He made his way over to the side gate, skipping up and down to keep from freezing. He liked his plimsoll-boots, wouldn't wear anything else being as how his dad said he couldn't afford exercisers like some kids had; but they weren't much good in the wet. His feet were soon soggy, and chilled. Come on, Shofiq Rahman, pull your finger out.

A few quick glances told him that Patsy Broome and Whitehead weren't around. If Whitehead was meant to be still off sick he wouldn't be daft enough to be seen near school, but he expected Patsy to be. They surely didn't think he'd go to Muscovy off his own bat did they, just to get a battering? The best thing to do was scarper, while the going was good. That would be the best thing, no danger. Maybe she was outside though, that was it, watching all the gates. If she wasn't – well, he just might.

She wasn't. But two of Bobby Whitehead's little'uns were, looking scared. He smiled nastily at them. Little-'uns were easy. He'd put the fear of Jiminy up them, for starters. Then he noticed someone else.

Although Bernard didn't know the girl, he half guessed immediately who she must be. She was a Pakistani, a couple of years younger than him, and she was dead pretty. She was dressed all up in silk pyjamas, and her hair was long and shining black, in a pigtail but not plaited. She was so pale she was almost like a white kid. But it was the cold, he reckoned. She was dressed like it was mid-summer. She looked frightened and sad, and he felt sorry to see her. She was belting looking, no question. He was certain who she was – Shofiq's sister.

Freddie Wright, one of Bobby's little'uns, said squeakily: 'You've to come to the Muscovy, Kershaw. Bobby Whitehead says so. He says he wants to tell you something!'

'He's got a dirty big stick, too,' chipped in Bertie Smith. 'He's going to half kill you, Kershaw. You go with Pakis!'

The last batch of Bernard's class were out. Maureen,

Dougie and Terry hung about, in two minds whether to be friends or not. Bernard scowled at them, and they went off. Maureen stuck her tongue out, but it was half-hearted, you could tell. Soppy bird, he'd let her sweat on it!

'You go and tell that silly twerp Whitehead to go and take a running jump,' he said. 'If I get hold of him he'll wish he hadn't been born, that's all. You tell him me and . . .'

Shofiq Rahman came through the gate, saw his sister, and jumped. He started jabbering at her in a foreign language, right fast, like total gibberish. He seemed angry, real upset. She put her head down and moved her toe in a puddle. She had on satiny sort of shoes, all soaked, and her pyjama legs were soaked too, stuck round her ankles. She spoke back, very soft. It struck Bernard as odd, even through the sinking feeling in his stomach, that they didn't speak English. How come they could speak two languages? It was smart, that.

But the sinking feeling got worse. He suddenly knew that he should have scarpered, that he'd done it all wrong. Sure enough, the Pakistani lad turned to him. After all the foreign jabber, his accent, just like Bernard's, was proper weird.

'I got to go, lad,' he said. Give him his due, he looked ashamed. 'Will you be all right? I really have. My sister – that's my sister . . . She's . . . Ee, hell, lad, I've got to scarper. Honest.'

Bernard bit his lip. The girl was still playing with her foot in the puddle. *She* didn't look upset. He didn't know what to think. Was it just a rotten excuse or what? He was miserable. He forced a smile.

'That's all right, lad. It were nowt any road. I'll be all right, you'll see.'

The Pakistani lad jabbered some more. He grabbed the girl's arm and started to pull her away, fast as fast. He flashed Bernard a look, like he was trying to smile. He opened his mouth to speak, then changed his mind.

'See you,' said Bernard. He felt a right berk.

He might still have got away with it if he'd done a bunk, but his pride kept him standing there till Shofiq had gone. It was quite some time before the Pakistani pair had turned a corner, and by then the inevitable had happened. Big Pat Broome, panting fit to bust, came rushing out of school. She nearly split her ugly mug when she saw him, she smiled so hard. She had a big blue mack on, like the kids down St David's wore. She grabbed his arm.

'We kept him, Patsy,' little Bertie Smith said, the little liar. 'He would've run off but we stopped him.'

'Yeah, he's right soft, ain't he,' said Patsy. 'Mr Ellis kept me in so he could get away I reckon. What a pansy you must be, Bernie Kershaw.'

Being called Bernie was the thing that Bernard hated most of all. Not many people dared, and anyone who did got put down in his little book for when Bernard the Black Hand got out his gun for the time of revenge. But for once, it was the least of his worries. As the four of them walked across the wet, muddy waste ground to the wreck of the Muscovy, he just felt totally miserable and depressed. Maureen and Dougie and Terry would at least have tried to stand up for him, probably, although they weren't much of a gang when it came to it. At least he could have got away from Patsy with them, though. But now everything was wrong. He was in for a battering, and it would be a good one. He was as miserable as sin.

# Chapter Seven

AT home that night, Bernard got no sympathy at all. He'd started off whining even before he got in the lobby of the flats, when he'd met his Auntie Mary coming out. He was sniffing already, and he put it on when he saw her, which was daft of him, because Auntie Mary was a right moaner herself, and she never listened to a word anyone else said.

'What's up with you then, Bernard?' she said. 'You look as if you've been in the wars. Ee, ruddy 'eck, it's cold out here, I hope your mother appreciates it, that's all.'

'It were some lads, Auntie,' Bernard started, but he didn't get chance to say much else.

'That sister of yours wants her bottom smacking if you ask me,' Auntie Mary went on. 'Staying in late at school with your mother in the state she's in. It's all very well saying she's got to pass her A levels, but what time have *I* got to come round cooking meals, eh? I've your Uncle Jeff to think of, too, you know, he'll be home soon and *he* won't thank me if there's nowt in th'oven.'

She hurried off, bent against the wind. Moaning old bag, thought Bernard. He hoped she'd miss her bus. Wendy, his sister, only stayed late at school about once a fortnight, and it was well known Uncle Jeff always went to the pub before he came home from the foundry and didn't take his tea until about eight o'clock, anyway.

He had to walk up to the sixth floor, where they lived,

because the lift was out of order again. He didn't mind that, because the stairs were open to the air in places, so they didn't stink of piddle and that as much as the lifts did. Up where they lived, right on the Yorkshire edge of the town, it was nearly always windy, because the moors and the mountains weren't far off. As you got higher up the flats the wind got stronger. It was smashing, the best thing about them. In his family's flat the wind battered and beat at the windows nearly all the time, even when it was practically calm down in the street. His mother said it got on her nerves, but Bernard loved it. It was smashing, living in a flat.

His mother was sitting in the kitchen when he pushed open the door, drinking a cup of tea and glancing at the paper. She looked pale, and sick, and for a moment or two Bernard almost forgot his own troubles. She looked so old and tired these days, did his mum, and only a year ago, or even less, she'd been a real sparky sort. She was taking pills now, that made her sort of dozy, and dopey, and Wendy did most of the work around the place, the cooking and cleaning and such. She smiled when she saw him though.

'Hello, love. Did you have a nice day? Ee, Bern, you've left footmarks all over the floor, you bad lad.'

He didn't bother to tell her anything that had been happening. She didn't listen to a lot of what he said, she was more interested in glancing at the paper or staring out across the town, counting the mill chimneys or something. Sometimes, he'd noticed, she actually held the paper upsidedown, and it didn't worry her. Once upon a time, before the do with the baby, she'd read a lot, the flat was always full of magazines. Now she didn't care.

Bernard poured himself a cup of tea and went to sit on the lav. He didn't really want to go, but he liked to sit there. He felt very lonely, really sad, looking at himself in the mirror on the bathroom door, supping his tea. By rights he ought to be in hospital, but it was no help that he wasn't. Bobby Whitehead was putting it off, that was all. He wanted it to be a real battering when it came, a proper gang thing. Bernard felt no joy at all because of his escape.

When the four of them had walked over the bridge thing into the outside yard of what was left of the Muscovy, Bobby Whitehead had been nowhere to be seen. Bernard had been flooded with relief. Perhaps he'd got bored, decided to go home. Patsy Broome was puzzled, too. But she jerked him along by his arm, right into the old weaving shed, shouting out Bobby's name. It was a scary place, where loose bricks sometimes dropped down off the high walls without warning. About three months ago a kid had broke his leg in there, when he'd slipped down an old shaft. Like everywhere else, they weren't allowed to play in it, because it was dangerous. But no one bothered to board it up properly, so everyone went in. A lot they cared, really, the grown-ups. They were just talk, that's all.

He was truly beginning to reckon he'd been let off the hook, that Whitehead had bombed off somewhere, when he was punched, very hard, in the soft part of the back. He screeched, because it hurt like anything, and Bobby Whitehead laughed loud into his ear.

'Fooled you, Kershaw!' he sneered. 'You thought I'd gone home, didn't you? You thought I'd chickened out, didn't you?' He poked him in the stomach with a hard finger. '*You're* the only chicken round here, kid. You dirty little blackie lover.'

Tears were washing round the bottom of Bernard's eyes, but he didn't think they showed. He was quite good at hiding it when he was crying, until it went past a certain point. He said nothing though. Safer to say nowt; pointless to open your trap.

'Whee,' said little Fred Wright, like the fool he was. 'You don't half look awful, Bob. You looks like a blinking ghost.'

Whitehead hit *him* then, not very hard, and Freddie started to cry. Whitehead hit him again, harder, to shut him up, and Bertie Smith started blubbing too. It would have been quite comical, little'uns were such a rotten nuisance, if it hadn't been today. Bernard kept his gob tightly shut.

'Go on!' said Bobby Whitehead, savagely. 'The both of you. Sod off, just gerrout of it. You give me a right pain you do!'

'But Bobby,' blubbered Freddie. 'You said . . . you said we . . .'

'Shut up and clear off!' shouted Whitehead. 'If you says one more word, just one, you're not in my gang no more. Out! Go! Sod off!'

Big Patsy and Bobby Whitehead looked at each other as the little'uns scarpered, and Bernard looked at Whitehead. His head was in a big bandage, all dirty it was by now, and he was proper pale. That Shofiq lad must have jolly near killed him after all. Oh what a *pity* it hadn't of been a lump of lead pipe, and not just rubber. What a crying shame!

'More trouble than they're worth, them twerps,' said Pat. She hitched up her skirt under her mack. 'What we going to do with Bernie then, Bob? Shall we smack him up then?'

Bernard looked full at Bobby Whitehead's pale and dirty face. He was about to accuse him of cowardice, two against one, but he changed his mind. He didn't dare.

'No fear,' said Bobby. 'We're going to tell him what for, that's all. We're going to give him fair warning. We're going to let him know just exactly what's going to happen to him for going with that smelly blackie.'

He was a big lad, Bobby Whitehead, and he was dead rough and a bully. Even being ill – and he definitely was ill, he wasn't half as vicious and frightening as he could be – he managed to make Bernard shake with terror. He told him that he was going to get some more big kids in,

58

Sammy Woods and Peter Winterbottom and a few of the other bad lads. They didn't often go together, because whenever there was a big brick fight they were usually on opposite sides. But Bernard knew they'd all get together for the fun of smashing him up, him and his mates. Bobby Whitehead told it slow, with all the gory details, and he could already see himself in hospital. And just to make it worse, Bobby said he'd never know when it was coming.

'We're going off to see Sammy now, me and Pat,' he said. 'It's time for us tea, but that can wait. You know Sammy, don't you, Kershaw? He loves to torture little gets like you. And he hates Pakis. We *all* do, and so will you after this little lot. Right?'

Bernard said nothing until Big Patsy twisted his arm. She got it right up behind his back till he screamed.

'Go on,' she said. 'Say it. "I hate Pakis"!'

No point in playing about.

'I hate Pakis,' he muttered. And under his breath: 'And I hate you, too, you big fat ugly dirty filthy smelly bitch.'

'Shall I make him cry, Bob?' said Patsy. 'I could you know, he's dead close.' She was grinning.

'Nah, leave him be,' said Bobby Whitehead. He rubbed his bandage, shaking his head. 'Listen, come on, let's find Sammy Woods and his lot.' He sounded tired. 'Go on then, Bernie Kershaw! Scarper off. And remember, pansy-face – we're going to do you, and it won't be long. What Mr Ellis reckons on doing to me because you split ain't *nothing* on what's going to happen to you. And the worse I gets it, the worse you'll suffer, see? You'll wish your mum had never bothered to have you.'

He'd left. He'd tried to walk off quite slow, as if he didn't care much. But Patsy Broome had hit him round the head with a big lump of wood she'd picked up, and then he'd run, so they couldn't see him crying.

During tea, which was a sort of manky hot-pot thing, that Auntie Mary had made in about ten seconds flat and

59

bunged in the oven, judging by the taste of it, Bernard had tried to tell them about it, but again he'd got nowhere. Wendy was in a bad temper, and kept banging down her fork and muttering about the taste of the food. Mum sat there sort of staring at the wall, and Dad, still in his overalls, was going on and on about some problems they were having at the mill where he worked. He was in the union, a big noise, called a shop steward or something, and he reckoned there was a lot of trouble coming, and it wouldn't be long about it, either.

'Are you following, love?' he said to Mum at one point. 'What I'm saying is serious, you know. It could mean redundancies, a lot of redundancies, up to a hundred maybe.'

'Oh dear,' said Mum. 'Is that right, love? Oh dear, it's just one thing after another, it seems to me.'

'Aye,' said Dad. 'And you'll be in trouble, our Wendy, if it comes to it. There's little enough money comes into this house as it is, what with you and your ruddy A levels and all. You'll be out looking for a job right smartish if worst comes to the worst.'

Wendy muttered something quiet. Dad banged on the table with his knife.

'What was that you said?' he asked, in a dangerous voice. Bernard's stomach went tense. His dad and their Wendy rowed a lot these days, they never seemed to stop.

'Oh nothing, Dad,' said Wendy. 'I just said "Give over". I didn't mean it, I'm tired.'

'*You're* tired! I like that. Been sitting in school all day reading books and *you're* tired. And here's me with the threat of the sack hanging over me, and *you're* tired.'

Wendy was a red-head, and she had a temper on her you had to see to believe. But she said nowt this time, and just spooned some more food on her dad's plate.

'I'm sorry, Dad,' she said. 'Is it honestly that bad?'

'That's right, dear,' said Mum, smiling. 'Eat up your tea, you won't be so tired.'

Dad sighed.

'Well it's this bad, anyway,' he said. 'I reckon we'll lose eighty jobs. Cheap imports, bad management, plant that were made in the 1890's, some of it. It's a bad do, it is that. Textiles in this country are in the mire. The industry's dying on its feet.'

There was a pause.

'Dad,' said Bernard, in a whiny tone. 'Can I stay off school tomorrow? There's some lads, a gang. They're going to batter me.'

'Oh shut up moaning, our Bernard,' said his father. 'Aye,' he went on to Wendy. 'Eighty jobs in next month or so. Maybe next couple of weeks. It's a problem.'

His mother said: 'But will you lose *your* job, dear? I mean, you're the union, aren't you? They can't sack you, can they?'

Dad laughed.

'Don't fret, love,' he said. 'I'll be all right. Nay, it's the fog inspectors who'll get it first, poor beggars. Still, it can't be helped.'

Wendy looked puzzled.

'Fog inspectors? What's them when they're out?'

'The Pakis,' said Dad. 'The night shift. Our brown brothers from overseas.' He spat out a piece of gristle. 'Fog inspectors we call 'em. Although I'm blowed if I know why!'

'But you can't let them be sacked just because they're Pakistanis, can you?' she said. 'I mean, surely them what's had the job the least time gets the sack, whatever their colour, that's the rule isn't it? I've done trade unions in current affairs.'

Dad nearly fell off his chair laughing.

'Oh aye, what haven't you done in current affairs?' he yelled. 'But believe me, lass, it's them that's out, if anyone is. We've got to look after our own, eh? If they don't like it, they should have stayed at home.'

For a minute or two it looked as if there was going to

be a fight. Wendy went red, all her freckles sticking out, a dead queer colour. She opened her mouth and said : 'Well it sounds rotten diabolical to . . .' Then she trailed off. She stood up and started snatching the plates off the table. 'Come on, our Bern,' she said, viciously. 'Get helping with the washing up.'

'I want to talk to me dad,' he whined. 'There's some lads in school . . .'

His father glared at him.

'Get helping and shut whining,' he said. 'I'm for telly. Come on, love,' he added to Mum. 'I'll settle you in your chair. Have you had enough dinner ?'

But later on Bernard did get a talk with his dad. He told him about the threat, and he cracked on a bit about how he'd stood up to them but there were too many of them. He told him all about the way they were going to batter him, and how Bobby Whitehead was such a big bully. Strangely though – and it did strike him as strange – he said nothing about Shofiq. Fog inspectors. What a funny name. He was half-ashamed about not mentioning Shofiq, but it seemed sense somehow.

Bernard's father, who he happened to know was thirty-nine next birthday, which was in July, had done some service in the Army. In the Army, the best thing that had happened to him had been the boxing. He'd been some sort of a champion, and he had three cups on the sideboard, two big ones and a little one, and four shield things as well. He put his arm round Bernard's shoulder and talked to him for quite a long time about what he should do, and he made it sound easy, absolutely simple, a complete and utter walkover.

The first thing to remember was that all bullies were cowards. One good crack and Bobby Whitehead would go down like a sack of cement, like a house of cards. Bullies also didn't like having their faces marked, because they were pansies and very vain (whatever that meant), so you always had to aim for their face. Then there was the golden rule: always attack. If he attacked when he saw the chance, if he waded in before Bobby Whitehead had got a gang together, when he wasn't expecting Bernard to do anything, there'd be no contest. He could knock Whitehead from Afghanistan to breakfastime, his father said, and that would be that; a piece of cake.

One thing he promised. If Bernard did what he said, if he followed all the rules his dad laid down, and kept his guard up into the bargain, he couldn't possibly get hurt. Whitehead would be routed, Bernard would be a hero, and there'd be no more bullying at all. Simple.

Bernard took off his jeans and jersey at bedtime and got into his submarine. He kept his socks on, although he'd promised Wendy he wouldn't because of what they did to the sheets. It was cold, so that made it just good sense, when all was said and done; she wouldn't want him to freeze to death in the night. When his mum had kissed him goodnight, he pulled the watertight hatch up over his head and got ready to submerge, keeping an ear outside so that he could hear the wind roaring and buffeting at the bedroom window, high up the block of flats. It was a lovely sound, fantastic, just like it would be right in the middle of an Atlantic gale.

As he submerged, he remembered he hadn't thought about redesigning the engine so it wouldn't use up all the oxygen. But for tonight it didn't matter. Not a German battleship did he see, not even a Russian spyship disguised as a trawler. He saw only Bobby Whitehead, and himself. And he battered him, and battered him, and battered him. It was fantastic.

# Chapter Eight

BERNARD had to do some really crafty tracking on his way to school to keep out of the way of the enemy. He crossed Middleton Road earlier than normal, where it came down the hill in a long right hand bend. Very dangerous, especially as there was a thin layer of snow over everywhere, and in fact he nearly got squidged by a dirty great truck. Its back was sliding about all over the show, despite the salting and gritting that had gone on in the night. A man on the pavement shouted at him, but Bernard the Black Hand just smiled a hard, mysterious smile and nipped up New Street. From there he made his way along the side of the estate, so that he came to the Jericho croft from a different direction from normal.

It wasn't Whitehead he was looking for, although he wouldn't have minded meeting him. He was bursting with power, and he knew that if he caught him on his own he'd be able to flatten him just like that, no trouble, with the tips his dad had given him. All bullies were cowards, anyway, that was the thing to remember. Sure enough, too, that rotten Shofiq had laid him out without any problem. Pity he'd never realised it before, because it would have saved him some right nasty dos.

No, the 'enemy' he was looking for was Maureen. Maureen in particular, and Dougie and Terry as well, who'd probably be tagging along with her. He had a jolly fair idea they'd be lying in wait, ready to ambush him, and he wanted to make sure they didn't get the satisfaction.

The danger-point was the top end of the road that curved left round the ruins of Jericho. Maureen could hide up there and get a good view across the croft, whichever way Bernard would normally approach it from. So he went high, right onto the edge of Datchett, where she'd have to come down. His nose was dripping and his feet were frozen, but Bernard didn't notice. He was in Siberia, on the track of the great Russian spy Ivan Odd-sok (a joke he'd got from the *Topper*) so you'd expect it to be ruddy brass monkeyish, wouldn't you?

Sure enough, as he passed the high walls of the Snipe, the posh new estate pub, he saw the three of them lurking behind a pile of rubble that had once been the Jericho gatehouse. They were all dressed up in winter togs, with Wellie boots on and long coats instead of anoraks. They looked daft, but that was their hard luck. His mum never noticed what he wore out any more, so he just had his fur-collar anorak and his plimsoll-boots on as normal. Better to be cold than look like a St David's kid.

He got himself into the doorway of a boarded-up shop out of the worst of the wind, to wait. He didn't know what time it was, but judging by the way some of the kids were pelting for the school gates it was probably quite late. Terry had a watch, which he was always flashing about, but Bernard reckoned it didn't tell the time right, because it never tallied with the school clocks. But he could see him look at it every now and then, and shake it, and hold it to his earhole.

They held on as long as they could. They must have been right choked. But there was no beating Bernard of the Black Hand when he was on the job. He gave an evil smile as they finally gave up and started racing over the croft, then set out to follow them, still keeping invisible, moving in quick bursts from cover to cover. By the time he got in, the buzzer had gone, and he got told off and made to stand at the back of the hall for prayers. Which meant that he was out first; and when Maureen and Terry and Dougie came into the classroom – there he was, sitting there. Their shocked looks made him grin behind his hand. Who did they think *they* were, anyway, trying to get the drop on him?

At dinner Bernard made sure he sat as far as he could from them, although Maureen had tried to hop smartly onto the same bench. So smartly, in fact, that she'd knocked over a water glass. It was a plastic one, and bounced, but she still got told off, as well as told to sit where she was, and sit still, and stop jumping about in a babyish fashion. So he ate his dinner alone, full of satisfaction, and decided when he'd speak to them.

After pudding, the time had come. He was bored with avoiding them, once he'd proved he could do it with no trouble, and in any case, Maureen often knew things that he didn't about what was going on in the rest of the school. And Bobby Whitehead, although his big turban bandage was gone, was looking pretty funny, and rumour had it he'd been caned black and blue by Ellis that morning. In any case, the only reason they'd been trying to get hold of him was to find out how he'd got on, and by now they should be almost frantic with nosiness.

He waited outside the hall door until they came out.

'Hiya, Maureen,' he said. 'Coming round the boiler room? I've got something to tell you.'

Maureen tossed her fair hair, trying to make her big blue eyes look vicious. They hadn't parted friends the day before, to say the least of it. Terry stood beside her, saying nothing. Dougie, the big twerp, opened his mouth and put his foot in it.

'You get lost, Bernard Kershaw,' he said. 'We ain't your friends no more.'

Maureen took her chance. She switched all her anger from Bernard to her brother. She punched him in the stomach, right over his tinned plums and school custard.

'Shut your stupid mouth, our Dougie,' she snapped. 'I'll tell you who you're friends with, see.'

'Come on, Ferretface,' said Bernard. 'I couldn't let you come with me yesterday, I had to have a word with Whitehead, that's all. If I'd took you lot along he might've said it was unfair.'

This bold statement, coupled with the complete lack of bruises and cuts such as they'd expected all over his mug, had the others goggling. They pulled on their coats and nipped round behind the boiler room. On their way, Bernard saw Shofiq trying to attract his attention. He'd tried it a couple of times, during the morning. But once again, Bernard ignored him. With friends like him, he thought, who needs enemies? A fat lot of good *he'd* been last night. Now he could stew, or fry himself, or turn into an air-balloon and float back to Paki-land. Bernard didn't want to know.

One good thing about the gang was, however much they'd fell out, once they got back together again there was no trouble getting started. No question of saying sorry or stuff like that. They listened eagerly while Bernard told them how he'd warned off Bobby Whitehead and Big Pat. He cracked it on quite hard, but he was so sure that the next time they met he'd be able to roll Whitehead up like a rotten carpet, that he sort of believed everything he said. He had them gaping a couple of times, and when he told them he'd made Bertie Smith and Freddie Wright run off shrieking, he genuinely saw himself doing it.

'I thought that Whitehead were looking a bit sick,' said Terry. 'I mean he *is*, no danger. But I thought that were because of what old Ellis done to him this morning, like Maureen said.'

'Aye,' said Dougie. 'You must have feared him proper, Bernard. Whee, he must have widdled himself.'

'Still and all,' put in Maureen, 'he did get a going over today though. Judith Wintle, what's in his class, told me

67

in playtime he'd been caned till he screamed blue murder. They had to have an extra music lesson to cover the screaming. It's true that,' she added, daring anyone to deny it.

That gave Bernard a slightly chilly feeling in his stomach, in view of what Bobby had said yesterday, in Jericho. If it *was* true, if Ellis had given Bobby a bad leathering, he'd be in a right nasty mood. He thought of the size of him, and his strength, and that beggar Sammy Woods, not to mention Patsy Broome. He called the boxing cups on the sideboard to mind: all bullies are cowards. But he didn't feel quite so sure, all of a sudden.

'Well,' he said awkwardly, trying to get back on himself just a little, just in case. 'I mean, I'm not saying he'll never be no trouble again, like. I mean, you know Bobby Whitehead. It might just come to a punch-up sometime. We might have to sort him out again.'

He thought he'd got in the word 'we' rather craftily there – so that if it came to it, in future, he could make sure the gang was there, to give him a lift, like. The others fell in quite happily, you could see that. Dougie's soft face was all jolly, as if he couldn't wait.

'Eh, that'll be great,' he said. 'We'll fix him proper, this time. Anyway, that Pakistani lad half killed him all on his own. We can finish off the job, like. Great!'

'Ah,' said Maureen. 'He's in lumber too, your Shofiq mate. Did you know that, Bern?'

Bernard almost said: 'He's no mate of mine', but something stopped him.

'How d'you mean?' he said.

Maureen smiled her happy smile. She was fantastic at getting to know things, and she loved to get one over Bernard. He didn't mind it from her, either. She'd've made a good spy, he didn't mind admitting it. She was a belter.

'They've had the Welfare in,' she said. 'Me mum were telling me dad last night.' Her eyes glistened. 'They're in real lumber, they are. The family's in a real bad way.

68

That sister of his, the one that wears pyjamas, she's always off school, she won't stay in. She gets bussed see, 'cause there's too many of 'em in our school, the council splits 'em up. And their mum's going round the twist. She's a right loonie.'

Bernard pursed his lips.

'So what's new?' he said. 'You told me all that before. Everyone knows that.'

'Yah,' said Maureen, sticking her tongue out. 'Everyone doesn't know that. My mum's a dinner lady; she gets to hear all sorts.'

Dougie nodded proudly.

'She's right nosey is our mum,' he added. 'That's where our Maureen gets it from.'

Terry, Bernard and Maureen laughed, which obviously puzzled Dougie, because he didn't know he'd said anything funny. He blinked. Then Maureen said: 'Anyway, Cleverclogs, I bet you don't know this: that Shofiq lad's in dead trouble, too. There!'

Now this *was* new. Bernard wiped his nose on his sleeve, casually. Maureen said nothing, so he had to ask, despite himself.

'Go on then, Slobberchops,' he said. 'I'll believe you, thousands wouldn't.'

'Well it stands to reason,' said Maureen. 'I mean all right, so Bobby Whitehead shouldn't have been bunging bricks at the curry kids, anyone knows that. But steaming heck, Bern, that pal of yours near killed him. Another inch, Judith Wintle says, and it'd have been a brain surgeon job. He were dead lucky, that's all.'

'Aye,' said Terry humorously. 'Anyone whose head wasn't as thick as Bobby Whitehead's would've been a dead'un.'

'More's the pity,' said Dougie. 'There ain't no justice.'

Bernard whistled. He'd never thought of this.

'Well go on,' he told Maureen. 'So what's happened to Sho— to the Paki lad? Is he to be caned as well? When?'

'Is he heck as being caned,' said Maureen. 'It's against the law to touch a Pakistani, don't you know nothing? Something to do with their religion or summat, I don't know. You can't touch 'em.'

'Not fair, I call it,' said Dougie. 'My dad reckons . . .'

Bernard interrupted. There was no time to hear about Dougie's boring dad.

'Well, what then?' he demanded. 'You said he were in trouble. Well, what trouble?'

Maureen looked doubtful, then relieved, because the buzzer had started to go, across the playground.

'He had to see Ellis, that's all I know,' she said. 'I think he were going in after his dinner or something. I don't know what they'll do. But they can't cane him, that I do know. It's against the law.'

'It's not fair, is it, Bern?' said Dougie. 'I wish I was a ruddy Paki.'

Sure enough, Shofiq came into the classroom nearly fifteen minutes after the lesson had started. He looked a bit queer, even quieter than usual. Bernard was eaten up with curiosity, and when playtime came he cornered him as smartly as he could, warning off the others with a glare and a lift of his eyebrows. 'I'm going to interrogate the suspect,' his look told Maureen. 'I'll see you after.'

All that morning Bernard had been avoiding Shofiq, who'd been trying to talk. But now Bernard wanted to talk to *him*, he seemed to have changed his mind. Bernard stood close, so that he couldn't get away without pushing past, and waited. Shofiq said nothing.

At last Bernard sort of coughed.

'Where were you then, last night?' he said. 'I thought you were going to give us a lift, you know, if it came to a fratch with that Whitehead.'

Shofiq kept his eyes on the floor.

'Sorry,' he said. 'I had to go. My sister . . .'

'Aye,' said Bernard, in a sympathetic voice. 'They're a ruddy nuisance, are sisters. I've got one of 'em myself.'

He stopped, but Shofiq did not respond. After a pause Bernard said: 'Did you see Ellis? Did you get in trouble? You know, because you battered Whitehead? Did you get the stick?'

'No one gets the stick,' said Shofiq, in a dull, tired voice. 'We're too young. It's only for show.'

Bernard was taken aback. That was daft! What about Whitehead, and the screaming, and the music lesson? He was about to protest, when Shofiq started to talk again. He sounded real bad, like he was about ninety years old. He sounded pig sick.

'He's told the Welfare,' he said. 'The Social Service man. And he's already been on our . . . He's got no right, it's not fair. I don't know what my mum'll say this time, it's getting to be . . .'

He tailed off, still staring at the floor. Bernard swallowed. He didn't know what it all meant, this talk of Welfare, and Social Services. He needed to hear more.

'It were that Whitehead,' said Shofiq bitterly. 'It were nowt to do with me. That Whitehead started it. And now what? I'll bloody kill the sod I will, I'll bloody kill him.'

He moved off suddenly, leaving Bernard standing there, gawping. Bernard was disturbed, and half excited. He kept a close eye on the lad for the rest of the afternoon, determined to talk some more after school, half expecting him to disappear into thin air.

That was more or less what he did do. To Bernard's fury, Miss Todd let Shofiq out in the first batch, and Maureen, Dougie, Terry and him in the second. By the time they got into the playground, he was a hundred yards down the road.

That was no problem, they could easily have caught him up. But what was a problem, and a shock, was that he was not alone. He was with a man, a short, very thin, Pakistani man, who must be his dad. They were walking fast, with their heads bent against the cold wind.

'Well, that's that then,' said Maureen, who was inclined to be fed up with the speed with which Bernard had tried to drag them out after the lad. 'His dad's come for him so you can't collar him anyway. I'm off home, it's rotten freezing.'

Bernard was in two minds. It was cold, and it would soon be dark, and he was hungry. But his curiosity was up. The lad had acted so strange. And now his dad being there. He wanted to *know*, he wanted to find out what was going on.

'All right, Softie-pants,' he said. 'You get home to Jackanory like a good little girl. But *I'm* going after. *I'm* going to track 'em down. I want to find out *just* what's what, that's all.'

They were amazed. They were aghast. After a couple of seconds Dougie said: 'You're going to *track* 'em? But they live down the Brook!'

The others nodded, with round eyes. Bernard laughed bravely.

'That's right,' he said. 'And that's where I'm going.'

'You don't *have* to come,' he added, after a pause. 'I don't *expect* you to come. After all, you *are* just a bunch of soft kids, that's all. But I'm going, so there. And I'm going now.'

He turned on his heel with a sneer, pulling his furry hood round his cold face. He set off at a good speed, to show he wasn't afraid. But he was really. He was petrified.

# Chapter Nine

SAY this for the gang, Bernard thought a couple of minutes later, they were prepared to have a go. He hadn't gone much more than a hundred yards, and he was slowing up pretty rapid, when he saw out of the corner of his eye, as he glanced over his shoulder, that the three of them were coming after. He felt good about that, dead good. He wasn't quite sure, to be honest, that he'd have gone on, if they hadn't come too. But they were coming. He got to the Musicians, then he stopped. A few ticks later they came up with him.

'Well well,' he said, rather like a teacher might have done. 'Changed your mind have you then? Decided not to be so chicken?'

Dougie was shamefaced, but Terry just grinned.

'You just watch it, that's all, Kershaw,' he said. 'We might change us minds again, then you'll be in trouble, lad.'

Bernard stuck out his bottom lip. Maureen, to avoid a silly argument, put on an act.

'But, Bern,' she said, all scared-like. 'You can't mean it? Not go down the Brook? Not now! It's night-time. It'll be dark soon!'

Terry looked at his watch. He held it to his ear, as usual, then shook it.

'It don't half get dark early,' he said. 'According to my watch it's only dinnertime!'

Dougie giggled; they all felt better. In fact it couldn't

73

have been much after four, if that, because of just leaving school. But it was a rough day, with low cloud, and it would soon be like pitch. It was daft, Bernard's idea, even he knew that.

'Come on,' said Maureen. 'Let's forget the whole thing. We can track him some other time.'

But Bernard had made his mind up. He wanted to know. Especially now Shofiq's dad was in it. He wanted to find out for sure what was going on.

'Shut your face, Maureen,' he said. 'If you're going to scarper, scarper. Me and the lads are going down the Brook. That's that.'

Maureen took the challenge.

'Yah,' she said. 'If you can do it, Bernard Kershaw, don't think I can't. I might be a girl and all, but I'd give you a run for your money, no danger.'

Terry shivered.

'Way you lot are going on,' he said, 'we'll not find 'em anyway. They've got miles on us now, miles. Are we going or aren't we?'

When it came to it, they were. They could still see Shofiq and his dad, although they were way down the street by now. That was one thing – grown-ups tended to use roads, instead of slutching through muddy crofts and so on. It not only made them easier to follow, but it made going down the Brook that much safer. At least there were street lights, and shops, and people, and cars. They weren't likely just to disappear off the face of the earth, like white kids sometimes did that went into blackie-land on their own.

For all that, though, by the time they got to the edge, to the street that was reckoned to cut off good old England from Little India, Bernard was sweating on it, and so, he knew, were Maureen, and Terry, and Dougie. They stopped under a street lamp. It was alight now, because the dusk was so thick it was almost night. Just opposite them was a greengrocer's, a Pakistani one, where the

74

vegetables were all peculiar and the man that ran it wore a white silk thing on his head and a sort of dress instead of trousers and a jacket. Dougie was a queer yellow colour in the lamplight, with eyes like big black shadows.

'Whee, Bernard,' he said, biting his lip. 'I'm right feared me, I don't care who knows it!'

It was useful, having one duck-egg like Dougie in the gang, because his soppiness made the others brave. Maureen thumped him and Terry called him a scared-cat. Bernard felt better as well: if Dougie was chickening out already, there couldn't be much to worry about; he was afraid of his own shadow.

'Aw come on, Doug,' he said, all chirpy. 'We've not been popped in the curry pot yet, you know. Anyway, look about, lad; there's dozens of white folk all over. They're not Jack the Ripper, you know! They won't eat you!'

As they got deeper and deeper into the streets, though, there was less talk. Down here in Little India, on the road down the Brook, the worst bit of all, it was somehow darker, and drearier, and scarier, than in their own parts of town. There were more street lights alight, because they didn't get smashed up the way the ones down Bernard's way did, but they were old-fashioned, like a bulb in the sitting-room, in funny little glass bubbles, and they didn't chuck out much glim. There were still lots of folk about, because it was early, only tea-time, but the white faces got fewer and farther between. All the women wore long clothes, like wedding dresses, and bits of cloth over their faces, and some had jewels stuck in their noses. There weren't many cars, and no bikes at all. In fact there weren't many people, not as many as you'd have got on Maureen's estate, or by the flats where Bernard lived. Still, it was cold, ruddy perishing, and they did come from a hot country.

They were only two street lamps behind Shofiq and his dad, now, tracking nice and easy. Because the lamps gave out so little, just barely lighting up the pavement and the fronts of the terraces and a patch of road, it was easy. Each time they got under a lamp, they waited till the man and the lad up front left the pool of light two ahead, then carried on. It was a piece of cake.

None of them had any idea where Shofiq lived, but they'd worked out a fair picture of where they were. They'd come off one of the big main roads, with the big old brick houses with glass porches, and were going down a street of small, flat-front houses with no front gardens. One behind this road was another one just like it, and behind that was the long flat expanse of the park. Bernard and the others still played in the park, on the far side though, and they approached from another direction altogether, so as to avoid Little India. Nobody used the rec at all, for the same reason, and in fact it was closed down, with no chains on the swings and just stumps of iron in the concrete where the roundabouts had been once. It was a pity, but you couldn't be too careful. Nobody wanted to end up in the deep-freeze at the Calcutta Restaurant.

Halfway down the street they were on, and luckily in a patch of streetlight, Shofiq and his dad suddenly turned left and disappeared. Bernard and Co put on a gallop till they came up to the spot. Then they stopped, afraid.

It was a little back alley, what his mum called a ginnel, between two blocks of the small terraced houses. It led through to the next road, and it was as black as the Ace of Spades. In the light shining at the other end, they could see the Pakistani lad and his pa crossing the road.

'Ee, that's that,' said Dougie. 'I aren't going down there, not for owt, lad! You're on your own now, Bernard Kershaw. No, not for owt!'

It was a right hairy one, no danger. They all looked at each other. Anything could be lurking down that alley, anything.

76

Maureen, for some reason best known to herself, gave a sudden giggle.

'Yah, you're soft,' she said. And she ran down the alley without another word. When she appeared in the light at the other end, the three boys pelted like mad, to pretend they'd not hesitated. But Bernard felt a right fool, and he was shaking. It wasn't much of a consolation – although it was some – to see that Maureen was as white as a sheet, and trembling like a leaf.

'You're potty you are, our Mo,' said Dougie crossly. 'You could've got us all killed!'

Bernard looked up and down the street.

'But where are they?' he demanded. 'Where's that ruddy lad, then? Blinking heck, Maureen, you could've kept your eyes open!'

They wandered up and down the narrow street for quite a while. There were lights on in most of the houses, and every one looked the same. Just a long row of old front doors, one window downstairs, one up. A few cars parked outside, not many. When they got to the end they saw it was called Cardigan Road.

'I wish I had a cardigan on,' said Maureen morosely. 'I'm right starved. Froze.'

They walked back, scaring themselves with stories about what would happen if they were caught. Dougie was sure they'd be eaten, and Terry sort of confirmed it by reporting what he'd heard his dad and a mate talking about only a couple of weeks ago. They'd been talking about funerals, because this chap worked for a joiner and he made coffins.

'You think of it,' said Terry darkly. 'Just you think. How often do you see a funeral, eh? Dozens of times, hundreds. Heck, I've been to two in my family alone. Well what colour are they? Eh, what colour funerals have you ever seen?'

They all thought about it. The general idea looked like the truth.

'That's right,' said Terry. 'That's just what this fellow

77

told me dad. *Have you ever seen a Pakistani funeral?* Eh? Well have you? No, you ruddywell haven't. See! That's it!'

Nobody spoke, but Bernard's mind was going like a mill engine. In a street lamp's glow they all huddled together. 'So what happens to 'em?' said Dougie at last. 'Where do they go? When they die? Ee hell, Terry . . .'

Bernard was just about ready to scarper when the car came along. They moved out of the pool of light in case it was a murderer on the look-out for some nice juicy white kids. The car passed slowly, a pale blue Ford Cortina it was, and stopped. The door opened and a white man got out. He looked along at a couple of front door numbers, then walked up to one not far away. He knocked.

There was something about him. He was quite short, on the plumpish side, with dark trousers and a sheepskin coat that came down just past his bottom, with a furry collar. He was carrying a briefcase and had a daft little hat on his head, like a Russian on the telly.

As the door opened at last, Bernard whispered: 'That's their house. I bet you. That's the man from the Welfare. He's come to see about Shofiq doing Bobby Whitehead.'

By now, the others didn't give tuppence farthing if it was the Man in the Moon. They were cold, and scared, and hungry, and fed up.

'Ooh great,' said Maureen nastily. 'Sherlock Ruddy Holmes strikes again. Well he's gone in now, Sherlock, so that's that. *We're* going home.'

'No, hang about a bit,' said Bernard eagerly. 'Let's go round the back. Let's peep in and see if we can see 'em.'

They couldn't believe their ears. Had he gone off his rocker? Bernard began to hustle them across the road, to where another alleyway, wider this one, led behind the houses to the park. They tried to resist, but he was determined, excited.

'Just a look,' he said. 'Come on, just for a second. I tell

you what, you just wait at the back for me, and I'll nip in myself, into the garden. I just want a look, that's all.'

There was no arguing with him. He had them all in a pile, by the wide alleyway. They didn't know what to say. He was barmy.

Bernard had actually got them into the alleyway and gone further down to sniff around when a door on the opposite side of the road opened. In the light of it a Pakistani man came out. He was small, with dark greasy hair, and a yellow, gingery, suedette jacket on, like the Welfare man's only pretend, not real sheepskin. Behind him, in the house passage, they could see a lady in long robes and a sort of veil. The door closed and he stood outside, looking up and down.

The kids were rigid with fear. As they stood there another door, two along, opened up. Another man came out, almost exactly the same, small, and dark, and in a thin, cheap coat. He was carrying a package. About five seconds later another door opened, then another. There was the sound of an engine, bigger than a car, some sort of a truck. It was coming along the road.

Maureen, Terry and Dougie were shaking with fear. They didn't know which way to run. Bernard, returning from a first glance at the tiny back gardens of the houses, saw their faces, saw the group of little brown men, and saw the mini-bus arrive.

'Oh,' he said. 'They're off on the night shift.'

But he was talking to himself. The others, without a word, had pelted off past him down the alley and onto the park. All the bogeymen *there* were forgotten. They'd forgotten, too, if they ever cared, that they were not allowed near the park at night under any circumstances whatever, because of the dirty old men. They were flying, and Bernard could hear their feet and their panting breath. He shook his head in wonder. What a gang of jerks!

To say he wasn't scared would have been a downright lie, but now he was there, Bernard decided to go through with it. The scene on the road was nothing to panic about, just the men getting in their mini-bus to go to the mill. A lot of the Pakistanis who worked nights organised mini-buses; he supposed it must be for cheapness or something, or maybe they went for a pint and a game of darts first. Anyway, it was obvious no one was out to cut his throat – it would make them late for clocking in. What's more, he'd really show them silly twerps if he went into the garden, and it might give 'em something to chew on. What a gang of useless, yellow, gutless berks!

The gate into Shofiq's backyard was half open, rotting on its hinges. There was a light on in the back room, but the curtains were drawn. As he passed the dustbins and the outside lavatory, he could hear babies screaming. Well, not babies maybe, he couldn't rightly tell. Little kids, certainly. And as he got closer to the house, yes, a baby too. They went on and on. No one seemed to be trying to stop them.

By the time he'd reached the back window, by the little coal-hole thing, Bernard was sweating cobs with sheer fright. If they had a dog he was done for! If someone opened the door! Oh heck, he should never have been here!

He edged up to the window, slower and slower. He moved his head sideways to the crack of light, where the curtain didn't cover. He put his eye to it and stared, waiting to be able to see, to get used to the glare.

It was disappointing, in a way. He didn't know what he'd been expecting, but it had to be more than this, it had to be. The kitchen, although very small, was just like any other kitchen, it could have been their own, before they'd moved off Haven Road to the flats. There was a table, sort of plasticky with spindly red legs, and a gas stove, a dresser thing with plates and cups, and a few chairs. There were people too, of course, and they were talking. He guessed they'd stayed in the kitchen because some food was getting cooked; there were two pots steaming on the cooker. There was the man from the Welfare, and there was Shofiq's dad, and there was Shofiq himself: these three were standing up.

Then he saw two others. One of them must be Shofiq's mum, although he couldn't see her properly, and the other one was Shofiq's little sister, that he'd seen the night before outside the school. They were much more interesting, and for a while Bernard couldn't take his eyes off them.

The mother was dressed up all in white, as if she was in a nightie. You couldn't see a bit of her, except her hands, that were pressed across her face, with lots of rings and bracelets on them. Even her head was covered, with a pinky, wispy thing, a kind of Woolworths scarf. She was sitting down, slumped down, leaning right forward in the kitchen chair. Somehow or other he thought she might be crying, from the way her shoulders were bent; but he couldn't properly tell. The little girl was standing by her, pressed up against her, with her arms round her, back and front. She was looking at the men, with her face just like he'd seen it the day before. Blank.

He couldn't hear what was being said. The Welfare man, although not tall, was much bigger than Shofiq's dad. He looked angry, nasty, sort of bossy. He kept waving a black plastic file, leafing through a sheaf of papers. Shofiq's dad had his eyes down, listening. And Shofiq, calm as ever, was translating, you could easily see that. He'd listen to the arm-waving man, then turn to his dad, then speak, then listen and speak to the Welfare. From upstairs the screams of the baby were absolutely terrific, deafening. The two little kids were bawling, lower but pretty steady. Funny that no one did nothing about it, he thought.

Suddenly Bernard realised that the man was going. He gathered up lots of papers and waved his arms about some more. Shofiq, still as cool as a cucumber, picked up a folder he'd dropped. His dad bent his back, as if he was bowing, pushing open the door to the passage.

Cripes, he'd left it too late! Bernard started to slide away from the window, fast but silent. Cripes, what if the bloke looked out the back, or anyone else! Crikey, he must've been mad, coming in here!

Even in his panic Bernard moved carefully and slowly. But once he was on the pathway he went like greased lightning. He'd almost made it to the gate when he tripped over an old set of wheels that he hadn't even noticed on his way up. He went flying, tripped again, and banged into the dustbins. At the same moment, the back door to the kitchen opened and a flood of light came out.

Bernard froze, thankful that he'd fallen between the dustbins and the lav. His heart was pounding but he didn't dare get up and run. He tried to control his breath, tried to make the panting quieter. The light disappeared as the door closed.

After a few seconds he heard footsteps. They were quite firm, straight down the path, not as though the person was searching for someone. Maybe he hadn't been heard after all. Maybe it was just someone going –

It was Shofiq. He saw him from beside the bins, in the dim of the winter garden. He was going to the lavvy, that was all. He still looked calm, calm and brave. Bernard admired him, he had to admit it. He was a real cool one.

When Shofiq had closed the lavatory door Bernard quietly picked himself up and started to creep round the bins and away. He was almost through the rotten old gate when he heard a sound that stopped him dead, dead in his tracks. He was utterly and completely shocked at the sound, shocked beyond belief. It was awful; appalling.

Shofiq Rahman was crying. He was howling and bawling his eyes out.

# Chapter Ten

BERNARD fell asleep that night, for the first time in ages, without ever having turned his bed into a submarine. As he'd undressed, as he'd crawled into the chilly pit and blown hot breath down inside to warm it up, he'd thought only of Shofiq. He was determined to get to know the lad; he was eaten up with curiosity about what was going on with the family, and behind his funny, secret-looking mug. He was still shaken, upset, by the episode of having heard him squalling. Crikey Moses, thought Bernard, I've never skriked like that, never in all my life. Things must be awful.

It was something to do with that Welfare fellow, the social worker or whatever, no doubt about that. Bernard thought about him, fattish and smug, real nasty somehow. He didn't know how Shofiq had kept so cool, talking all quiet like that when the bloke had been waving his arms about. What a funny do, eh? His mum sitting there all hunched up, and his dad sort of little, and kind of lost, as if he was the lad and Shofiq was in charge of him. Bernard hated the Welfare man; he could tell he was the trouble.

Dreams of terrorism, and bombing, and murder, drifted into his mind. Bernard the Black Hand and Shofiq Rahman, the Paki Peril. Between them they could sort it all out. Not only this Social bloke in his daft Russian hat and posh-looking sheepskin, but Whitehead's lot too. He'd read somewhere you made bombs out of sugar, although it didn't sound very likely, that. But he'd have to find out.

They could bomb the fat bloke's car; it was only a rubbish Ford anyway. Perhaps they could bomb Whitehead and that Patsy too – get 'em into the Daisy engine house or the Muscovy by a crafty ruse, then blow 'em up sky-high. He'd like to see Big Patsy's legs fly off.

The problem was, of course, how to pin this Shofiq lad down. As he walked to school, too preoccupied even to be a destroyer or a jet fighter, let alone a secret agent, Bernard realised it might be hard. If it hadn't been for him having seen Shofiq belt Bobby Whitehead they'd never have got to talk, and since that morning it'd been practically impossible. He seemed to have spent half his life, since, trying to get together with the lad, and it hadn't come off at all. He couldn't make up his mind whether Shofiq wanted it that way, or whether it was just bad luck. Maybe it was some of both.

For most of the day it looked like it would end up that way again. He got no chance to have a word with Shofiq during morning playtime, and at dinnertime he was no-where to be seen, which wasn't unusual. Bernard enjoyed himself enough, cracking on to the others about the danger he'd been in – how he'd been chased by ten big black men all over the park, how one of them had had a gun, he'd seen it glinting in a street light for sure – but he kept his eye open all the time, on the look-out for the lad. Maureen and Terry and Dougie, to cover up their shame at having done a bunk, rubbished him from a great height, calling him all the liars under the sun – but they were dead impressed really, green with envy. When they asked him what he'd seen though, in the garden, Bernard just put on his Secret Service smile. And he said absolutely nothing about Shofiq bawling, not a word.

Funnily enough, it was Miss Todd that gave him the opportunity to corner Shofiq, in fact you'd have thought she'd had it planned. They'd been doing numberwork for the first part of the afternoon, which always made a lot of the kids grumpy and fed up, so she thought she'd give them a treat, or a favour or something. It was a typical daft teachery idea – all the kids were to be paired off in different parts of the room, and sit and talk to each other. Not to anyone else, like, just to each other. They had to rabbit on about 'My family and friends'.

At first she reckoned everyone could choose their own 'partner', but she dropped that idea sharpish because of the chaos it was going to cause. She probably realised, a little late, that it would be like choosing sides for games: you always ended up with the fat, ugly, smelly kids that no one liked being left till last, and some of them were quite liable to bawl, which Miss Todd didn't like at all. Bernard got himself as close to Shofiq as he possibly could, and made it quite clear who *he* wanted to talk to. He needn't have worried either, because she pointed him out one of the first of all.

'Right, Bernard, you go with Shofiq there. Take the blue corner and keep your voices down. I'm sure you've got plenty to talk about.'

Shofiq nodded quietly and wandered off, followed by Bernard. Funny the way old Toddy went on, he mused. She'd obviously got him and Shofiq down as buddies, and she thought it was a real good thing. Funny the way you were meant to love people just because they was coloured; it didn't make sense.

Still, he was very glad it had happened. He sat down opposite the Pakistani lad, with the babble of voices and the scrape of chairs all round them, and gave him a grin.

'Hello, pal,' he said. 'She's daft that Miss Todd, ain't she? Call this work? I dunno.'

Shofiq smiled wanly and shrugged. He didn't say anything. Didn't even look as though he'd anything to say. Bernard was put out.

'Aye,' he said, after a pause that went on for ages. 'Well, here we are then. We're meant to be talking, you know. "My family and friends". Daft, I call it.'

Still Shofiq said nothing. Bernard glanced about. Most

85

of the others were chatting away nineteen to the dozen. Maureen was with Terry, which was a right waste of time! They lived two streets apart and had known each other since they were kids. He was getting nervy.

'Well,' he said, 'my name's Bernard Kershaw, like you know. Hadn't we better talk to each other, don't you reckon? How did you get on then? That what you were talking about yesterday, about Ellis? Did the Welfare man come then?'

The Pakistani lad turned big brown eyes on him. Blimey though, they *were* big. They were very calm.

'No,' he said. 'It were nowt. I were just a bit upset that's all.'

Bernard swallowed the lie without a murmur. No point in telling the truth unless you had to, he knew that. But he was vexed as well. He wanted to *know*, to hear things. He tried another tack.

'That Whitehead got a thrashing, though, whatever you say, like. There was an extra music lesson to cover his screaming. Judith Wintle said so.'

Shofiq got livelier.

'That Bobby Whitehead,' he said. 'If I get hold of him I'll . . .'

Miss stuck her nose in then, just when something was starting to get moving.

'Now now, boys,' she said. ' "My family and friends" if you please. Robert Whitehead is neither, as you very well know!' She laughed at her own joke. 'I want you to talk to each other about each other. I'm sure you, Shofiq, can tell Bernard something about the Asian way of life. So different, it will be very interesting. And you, Bernard. Tell Shofiq about . . . well, tell him about your family . . . and friends.'

There was dead silence after she'd gone. Teachers were a menace. Shofiq scratched his nose. At last he said: 'I wish I had a gang like you.'

It was a start. Bernard snorted.

'Oh, they're not a real gang,' he said. 'I mean, Terry and Maureen's all right, but Dougie's a pain. And when it comes to battering. You should've met my mate Mickie. *Then* it were a real gang.'

'I saw him around,' said Shofiq. 'He got run over by a train, didn't he? Last year?'

'Yeah, there was blood for miles. They took him down the hospital in buckets. He were smashing, a *real* mate. We don't do nothing now, 'cept go in the buildings and that. It's no fun no more.'

There was silence.

'What do *you* do, then?' he asked. 'I mean, who do you go round with?'

Shofiq shook his head, his eyes cast down.

'I don't do nothing,' he said. 'I don't get time. I got the kids to look after and that. My dad works nights, mostly.'

Bernard was excited. He was on the edge of discovery. He waited for Shofiq to go on. He'd tell about his mum now, for certain. Shofiq, however, had finished.

After a while Bernard said: 'Go on, then. I mean, I've told *you* everything. Why don't you go out to play? Why do you look after the kids? What's up with your mum?'

This was very daring, but still Shofiq didn't rise. He shook his head gently, still staring down.

'There's a lot of work with a baby and two little nippers,' he said. 'We're all kept pretty busy.'

Bernard knew that Miss Todd would be calling an end to this soon; it was pretty near home time. He was impatient, anxious because the golden opportunity was getting lost.

'Look,' he said, almost defiantly. 'Why don't you come in my gang? They wouldn't mind, and it'd be a good laugh. I mean, we don't do much now, but . . . it'd be a good laugh.'

Shofiq looked up, and his eyes had got much brighter; they almost glowed. His mouth opened slightly. He smiled.

Then it faded. He got a hunted look on him.

87

'Thanks, pal,' he said. 'That would be dead good. But I can't, honest. I ain't got the time. It's a fact.'

Miss Todd had called a halt. She was all brisk and orderly, sorting them out like soldiers on parade. Bernard was furious.

He said to Shofiq angrily, cruelly: 'Maureen says your mum's a nut-case. She's been in the loonie-bin.'

Shofiq jumped as if he'd been stung. His dark eyes went darker.

'Come *on*, boys!' shouted Miss Todd.

He said quietly: 'She's not a nut-case, she's been ill, that's all. It could happen to anyone.'

Bernard was so infuriated by his calmness, by the daftness of it, the lost opportunity of Miss Dopey Todd's potty half-hour, that he spoke again, almost a snarl.

'I heard you in the lav last night, kid,' he said. 'You were blubbering fit to bust. I were hid by your outside lavvy. I heard you.'

Shofiq's face had a stunned look, his gob was all open. Bernard was yanked backwards, yelling, with Miss Todd's talons in his earhole. He also got a slap round the cheek.

'Now, when I tell you,' she said furiously. 'If you're not careful, Kershaw, you'll be here till six o'clock!'

As it was, he didn't get let out till the last batch. Maureen and Terry had gone first, Dougie in the next lot, and Shofiq Rahman in the one before Bernard. The others were waiting for him, but he didn't want to know. He jumped through the gate, his eyes searching all over the croft for a sight of the green jumper.

'Eh up, Bern,' said Maureen. 'What's the ruddy blush? Where are you off to so sharpish?'

'Gerrout of it, Barmpot,' he said, shaking her hand off his sleeve. 'Which way did that Rahman go? I've got unfinished business!'

'Hee hee, get him!' said Dougie.

Bernard went wild.

'Listen, you daft gets!' he shouted. 'It's important! Which way did he go, did you see?'

Terry said: 'He went over New Earth way I reckon. He'll likely be going to cross over at Schofield Street. Eh Bern, what's up? Can we come too?'

Bernard was already running.

'No, sorry!' he shouted, over his shoulder. 'Thanks, Terry. I'll tell you tomorrow. It's just something, that's all.'

They started to trot after, in a half-hearted way. But he had his head down, going like the clappers. They dropped off after a minute or two.

The sky was lowering and already quite dark. The Jericho croft was all pits and puddles, and Bernard's speed meant he was soon covered in a spray of mud and water. When he got to the New Earth Street side, he looked all over, straining his eyes. He saw nothing, so pelted down as fast as he could. When he'd reached the third junction he caught a glimpse of green. He stopped, checked. It was him, it must be! He'd picked up the trail.

Bernard followed fast, using all his years of skill and cunning as a tracker. But they hadn't got halfway down towards the Brook before Shofiq rumbled him. He stopped, looked round, and saw Bernard just as he stepped out from behind a pillar box. They stared for about a second, then Shofiq started to run like a hare.

He was fast, as fast as Bernard, and after a few minutes it looked as if he might get away. He belted down the main road, in and out of the people, without ever looking back. When they got to the edge of the railway, he did a sharp left turn and into the graveyard of St Peter's. It was his best move yet.

When Bernard reached the churchyard wall, he hesitated. It was more or less dark now, but that wasn't the whole problem. St Peter's graveyard was haunted, worse haunted than any other graveyard in the whole area. It was also a direct route down the Brook, and all the blackies walked through it all the time. They didn't believe in God, see, so it didn't worry them; they presumably had their own ghosts to haunt 'em back in India. And they made sacrifices there, killed chickens and drank their blood and that. It was diabolical.

All this went through Bernard's head in a flash, and in a flash, also, he was up and over the wall. He raced between the cracked and tumbledown old tombstones like a little rocket, his heart hammering, panting madly, skipping from tomb to tomb as if the hounds of hell were on his tail. At last, between the trees and the great stone angel with a broken wing by the far wall, he caught a glimpse of Shofiq. He put on a mighty spurt.

It was a big graveyard, and disused now, and all bust up by bad lads and vandals. Bernard caught Shofiq because of this. He came racing past a big old tomb, with iron rails all round, and nearly fell over him. Shofiq was sprawled full length in the mud, with a tear down the leg of his jeans. There was blood coming out of a cut, you could see it in the dark. And he was crying again.

Bernard crouched down beside him until his breathing came back to something like normal. Shofiq was lying half on his side, with his head cradled in his arm. He wasn't crying noisily, not sobbing, but he didn't seem inclined to stop either. It started to rain, the water whispering gently in the bare branches of the trees.

After a short while Bernard felt about in his anorak pocket and found a quarter of a roll of Polos. He cleared the dirty paper off with his teeth and patted the crying boy on the shoulder.

'Have a Polo, Shofiq,' he said. 'I want to be your mate.'

# Chapter Eleven

BERNARD didn't understand a lot of what he learned from Shofiq over the next while, but that didn't matter much. What did matter, what made him feel great, better than he had done for ages, was that they became mates, buddyroos, real muckers. It was even more amazing, and good, because it came at just the right time; Bobby White-head and Pat Broome were getting uppity, they had something up their sleeve. Not very far up, either: it was as clear as daylight that revenge was in the air. There was going to be a war.

On the night Bernard helped Shofiq home from the churchyard they didn't say much to each other, just wandered along sucking Polos, with Shofiq limping and still sniffling from time to time. Once Bernard had hoicked him onto his feet, there was no question of him trying to run. Somehow it had clicked. They walked along easy, relaxed, as if they'd been pals for ages. Shofiq said to leave him at the end of the street, and Bernard didn't argue: everyone knew best about their own house, like. Before he turned away though, he did manage to say this:

'I'm sorry what I said about your mum, lad. I'm right sick. I were all steamed up because of that silly old crow Toddy.'

'That's all right,' said Shofiq. 'She's not been right for a bit, you know. It's . . .' He sniffed. 'She's not a nutter though. She's not been well. She'll soon be better. She's not a nutter.'

Bernard left, very thoughtful, but glad as well. He walked through Little India without even realising he was doing it, without even realising he should by rights have been leapt on and murdered, or ended up on the meat hooks at the Calcutta. It never entered his head.

He'd learnt about some of the problems Shofiq had to face when he'd taken him to the secret hide-out he had that no one else knew about. In a way, it was even better than his submarine, because it was an actual place, and not just his bed. On the other hand, though, it wasn't entirely his. Although no other kids knew about it, Maureen and Terry and Doug, it was also used by some older lads and lasses, when they had nowhere to go to do their courting. Not often, but you could never be sure.

As they walked to it for the first time, on a cold and sleety Saturday morning, he pointed out the other good places to Shofiq. The buildings that they went into every now and again, on the way to the flats. This new estate being built wasn't flats at all; because, according to his dad, the council had decided flats were not a good plan after all. This new estate was meant to look something like the good little stone terraces that used to be there, before they'd pulled 'em all down. Only difference was, the new ones were made of a nasty purply brick, with windows so little it would be like living in a cave. Bernard and Shofiq agreed that most grown-up people appeared to be off their rockers – because Shofiq lived in a good old little terraced house that was smashing, and Bernard lived in a tower block, which was absolutely fantastic.

'What I can't see,' said Bernard, 'is why they pull them down for starters. I mean, them stone places were dead good, Mickie lived in one. Stands to reason brick won't last like stone, anyway. One thing though – it's useful having buildings to go in – good fun. We don't do nothing bad, like,' he added. 'I mean, the bad lads and vandals, they smash up the windows and break the lavvy bowls and that. We don't though. We just play.'

When they got into the lobby of the flats, he could see that Shofiq was a bit shaken. He had to admit, looking about him, that it was filthy dirty, and the stink of piddle and that was terrible. You got some right dirty devils, no mistake. The walls were filthy too, covered in writing, and paint, and dirty words and pictures. He pointed out a big, two-foot high MUFC in red aerosol, with 'are a lot of fairies' written underneath, in felt-tip marker.

'I done that,' he said proudly. 'The felt-tip, not the paint. You got to be rich to have them squirter things. They're dead dear.'

The lift door was open, and it ponged something dreadful. But it wasn't working, so they walked. He could tell Shofiq thought the place was pig-dirty, and he was ashamed. His Uncle Fred, who was a gas fitter, had often told his dad how dirty-filthy disgusting Pakistanis' houses were, so he thought it was a cheek, in a way. But they were both very polite, no point in having a fratch. They stomped up the stairs in silence.

When Shofiq saw the hide-out, he changed his tune. It was hard to get to, you had to squeeze through a narrow concrete gap at the back of one of the stairwells, but inside it was smashing. At your back was a big dull aluminium duct affair, and it was warm. It was the metal duct that took all the heating waste out of the flats up to the roof. It hummed and vibrated if you put your back to it. And out of a gap quite high in the wall you could see for miles – right across the town, which was very high up, being built on the edge of the moors, right down the huge flat area beyond, with other towns dotted in it, right down to the purple smudge of Manchester. He told Shofiq this, and was believed, although today you could hardly see anything because of the snowy sleet and the low clouds.

'On a clear day you can see the C.I.S. building in

Manchester,' he said. 'Miles, that is, miles and miles and miles. But ain't it warm, eh? And it's real brass monkeys out.'

In various times in the hide-out, whenever they could get there alone, when Shofiq wasn't too busy with his family or they were out with the others, Bernard got to hear about his mum, and his dad, and his sisters and baby brother, and all the other things. Bernard told him about Mickie, he talked for ages sometimes, even though it made him feel real sad. He could tell Shofiq was glad, somehow, that he hadn't found this place till Mick was dead, and Bernard didn't mind after a while. He almost told him, a couple of times, about how he'd chickened out of going to the railways, so that Mickie had got killed alone. But it always stuck, at the last moment. The words wouldn't come out.

What the real problem was, for Shofiq, was this: Although they'd been in England for ages, years – all the kids had been born here, like – his mum still couldn't speak English. She wasn't thick, he added quickly, it was just the way it was. Because of having all the children, because of the neighbours they had, because she was shy, because of their religion, because of the way his dad thought women should go on. She never got out. She never got to talk to anybody. In the end, it got her down.

Bernard couldn't follow. Crikey Moses, they lived in a street full of Pakistanis, she had millions of neighbours. How could she be lonely?

Shofiq explained again and again, but he never really made Bernard understand some things. As far as Bernard could see they were all the same, all Pakistanis. In fact, Shofiq said, there were three separate languages spoken in their street alone, as well as English. And most of the other people, in his mother's eyes, were not the sort she'd want to know.

'But ruddy hell!' said Bernard at one point. '*Why?* You mean she's locked herself up and got all funny, ill

like, because she won't talk to the neighbours! It's bar . . .
Ee, Shofiq lad, I don't get it!'

Shofiq said quietly: 'It causes all sorts of problems,
right enough. There's me sister, like. The eldest. I suppose
most of this, most of the real trouble, the bad trouble,
were caused by that.'

Bernard pricked up his ears. He was interested in girls,
and this sounded juicy. But it wasn't. Again it was something daft, something simple. The girl had been bussed,
that's all. Not allowed to go to Shofiq's school, but picked
up every day and taken over to the other side of town.
What was wrong with that?

'This is what's wrong,' said Shofiq bitterly. 'We don't
get asked, that's what's wrong. They tell us. We're Pakistanis, and it's for our own good, and we don't get a
chance to say owt about it. They say it's for the future,
like, to mix us in. But we *are* the future. And my mum's
*now*, and it's made her right ill. When's she meant to get
better? When *is* the ruddy future?'

He stopped, got gloomier.

'My sister's never been right since she got took away
from our school, and they say it's for her own good. So
she'll be a better ruddy person. They don't know owt
about us, and they reckon they're doing it to help. I
wonder they don't just get bottles of bleach out sometimes and try to make us white like them. Instant Bloody
Paki Wash, 50p.'

Bernard fell about, but Shofiq wasn't laughing at all. He
said musingly: 'She spoke ruddy good English less than a
year ago, my sister. Now she don't speak it hardly at all,
now she's been moved for her own good. She don't hardly
speak *anything* at all. She's gone just like me mum.'

This sister, it turned out, had taken to skipping school
as well, partly on account of she hated it, partly because
of helping their mum look after the baby. That had led
to the truant man coming in, then the Welfare, then
that social worker. Shofiq's eyes blazed with hatred when

he talked about the social worker, whose name was Mr Burke.

On one occasion, Bernard had asked why his father didn't sort it out, why it was that he, Shofiq, seemed to do most of the coming and going, getting the wheels turning and all that. His father, he thought on the quiet, sounded a bit of a duck-egg.

'It's not his fault,' Shofiq replied. 'He don't understand, that's all. It's beyond him. Back home he were a fairly well-off man, I reckon. He were a textile engineer, right skilled, not a ruddy night shift labourer like now. He were respected in his trade. Now he's earning buttons, and there's a chance he might lose his job, and all the white folk at mill hate his guts, him and all the others. They do awful things to 'em, Bernard. Taunt 'em, and take the mickey, and nick their food packets and chuck 'em down the lavs. They're like kids, not grown men. Worse.'

'What did he come for then?' Bernard asked suddenly. 'I mean – why bother to come at all, eh, if he were so ruddy well-off? Why come to our country, like?'

A queer look came over Shofiq's face.

'You'll laugh,' he said. 'Someone told him streets were paved with gold.'

Bernard was at a loss. Was it a joke? He couldn't tell by looking; he didn't know. Shofiq's face was giving nothing away, it was blank. Bernard didn't dare ask again.

Then Shofiq added: 'It's true that, lad. That's what he always says, any road. He says your lot asked him to come, he were needed. They said the streets were paved with gold. That's a laugh that. A right laugh.'

Bernard looked at the closed face, then away.

'Well,' he stumbled. 'I mean . . . Don't he speak English though? I mean that time I . . . Well, you know, you sort of translate for him, don't you?'

'Oh aye, he can speak it all right,' Shofiq replied. 'But

96

English folk don't understand his accent. They don't try, mebbe. No, truth to tell, his accent's very hard. And he's got a speech do, an impedi . . . I don't know, he can't talk quite right, he lost half his tongue when he were a lad.'

'Were it a tiger?' asked Bernard eagerly. Shofiq looked at him, amazed.

'No,' he said. 'He ran into a glass door.'

Although Mr Rahman could speak English, Shofiq did admit that he didn't write or read it very well, especially write. So when it came to dealing with things, like gas bills, and income tax, and forms and all that, he had to do it for him, more or less.

'I go with him to offices,' he said. 'You wouldn't believe it, Bern, the way a lot of official folk treat us. It makes me wild. They're pigs, some of 'em, just pigs. And he says nowt, and takes it, and tries to speak proper and polite. I'd kill 'em if I got the chance, I would honest. I sometimes think of doing in that Burke, tearing his guts out with a knife. Or burning down the social work office, you know, Gateway House, over by the park. That's where they hang out, you know, the social workers. There and in town centre, in Century House.'

Bernard hadn't known, but he was interested. Gateway House, on the edge of the park, the opposite edge from down the Brook, was all on its own. He reckoned they could raid it dead easy. And it was old, too. It would burn like a torch.

In the gang, with the others, Shofiq was a completely different person. There was none of this sort of talk, none of telling each other secrets. It was all good straightforward messing about, and he was a real good member. He thought up lots of things to do, when he was there. When he was there, though: that was the only trouble. Lots and lots of times he had to miss things because of difficult dos at home and that. The first time, when he'd had to go off, there'd been talk of his loonie mum. But

Bernard, with a savagery that had shaken even him, had put that down. He'd smacked Maureen's nose in so hard that she couldn't even fight back, just stood there and bled.

The only other confrontation, when Bernard had got them all together to tell them Shofiq was 'in', was over the word Paki. Even Bernard hadn't realised that Shofiq hated it – he'd even addressed his first note to 'The Paki' he recalled with a blush – and at first he'd been inclined to laugh at it. But Shofiq was serious.

'I can't rightly explain,' he said, 'but it's horrible. I mean I don't call you lot all Whities, or something. There's just something . . . it sounds . . .'

'Ah rubbish, lad,' said Terry. 'Everyone calls Pakis Pakis. It stands to reason. I mean, my dad calls Pakis Pakis; and blackies. Like West Indian kids gets called niggers and Chinese is Chinkies. I mean, it's just what you get called, it don't mean nowt.'

'It does, it does!' said Shofiq. 'I'll tell you, it means . . .'

He was helpless. He couldn't explain.

'I just wish you wouldn't, that's all,' he ended lamely.

'Rubbish!' said Terry firmly. 'I'll call you what I like, and you're a Paki, so there.'

Shofiq started to push up his sleeves.

'All right then, Smelly White Pig,' he said grimly. 'Take your coat off, lad, 'cause I'm going to batter you.'

Maureen solved it in the end by pointing out that no one was allowed to call Bernard Bernie. Bern was all right, or even Slobberchops. But not Bernie. They discussed as to why, but he couldn't rightly say. But he hated it, and that was that. Terry, who wasn't thick, agreed that he'd not call Shofiq a Paki.

'It's not just me, though,' said Shofiq. 'Everybody hates it, it's rotten. But thanks, Terry.'

'Well I won't call any of 'em – you – Pakis in future,' said Maureen. 'Pakistanis is good enough for me.'

Shofiq giggled: 'Or Indians, or Bangladeshis, or Sri

98

Lankans, eh? How about British? It's on me birth certificate!'

But that just got them confused. In any case, Bernard wasn't too pleased with the way Maureen was making up to Shofiq. He was *his* mate. Anyway, perhaps she fancied him, and then he'd be jealous the other way maybe. So he started a good friendly punch-up to seal Shofiq's membership of the gang.

It was Shofiq's idea that they stop calling themselves just a straightforward gang and become guerilla fighters. They had some trouble with exactly what the word meant and how to spell it, so they decided to be gorilla fighters instead, like great big apes; it sounded much more fun, that was for certain. The main enemy was to be White-head and his lot, and their main tactic, at first, was to keep a close watch on them and everything they did. They knew he was cooking up something for the time Shofiq had laid him out and Bernard had backed him up, but now that Shofiq had joined the gang, he'd obviously decided he had to be right careful; once bitten, twice shy. What's more, despite several warnings from old Ellis, Shofiq had taken to standing on the Jericho croft some mornings as the little Pakistani kids went in, casually chucking a couple of rocks up and down in the palm of his hand, sometimes with Bernard not far away doing the same. The little kids must've thought it was their birth-days, or something, because neither Whitehead's lot nor any of the other bullies had been able to belt them up for ages. Bernard loved it. For days on end he gave up the Secret Service, and his Luger, and carried a Winchester '73 on the Texas cattle trails, watching over the herds of defenceless brown kids with his mate, Two Gun Rahman, who preferred Colt 45s.

Shofiq's ideas on attack were surprisingly similar to Bernard's dad's, and he had proved very well, that first time, just what a great charge, even on an enemy with more troops, could do. The band of gorillas kept their eyes peeled whenever they were out of school. One day they'd get Whitehead at a disadvantage. And then, why wait for him to get up a bigger gang than them? They'd just wade in, everything firing, and blast him off the face of the earth.

The day it happened it was snowing hard, and a policeman had been in the school warning them about an outbreak of vandalism in the district, so in a way you could understand the gang not being at its best. But it was still a crying shame, a rotten pigging shame, and a bit of a disaster as things turned out in the end.

They'd all met up after school and gone to the sweetshop to spend Dougie's money. He was a bit of a thick, was Dougie, but you had to admit he was no fool where brass was concerned. He always saved it when the others spent, and he always produced it at the best moment. They came away with their gobs stuffed with Peculiarly Strong Peppermints. Just the ticket.

Despite the weather they were going to walk up to the old quarry workings way up past Bernard's flats to see the crane that had fallen down there. It had been demolishing the quarry buildings over the weekend when one of its tracks had gone down an old shaft. It had toppled over, killing a man, and it was reckoned you could still see the blood and pieces of his bones. It was worth a trip.

About two hundred yards before they got to the buildings, though, the ones they played in, Terry – with just his eyes poking out of his balaclava – saw Bobby Whitehead. He was dressed in an old overcoat, that looked like it had once been his mum's, and he was with a great fat lump in a blue mac who could only be Patsy Broome. They couldn't believe their luck!

Dougie, the fool, the complete ruddy twerp as always, let out a great yell. If he hadn't, they would have caught up gradually and battered them whenever they'd wanted to. Now, instead, it became a chase. Whitehead and Patsy Broome stopped, looked over their shoulders, looked at each other – and bolted. Bernard, Shofiq, Maureen, Terry and Dougie all shouted then, and carried on shouting as they took up the chase.

It was snowing like billioh, right into their faces, and they were running uphill. Well slithering, more like, slithering and slipping like a bunch of lousy ice-skaters. By the time they'd reached the boundary fence of the buildings, Whitehead and Patsy had gone. Straight through a gap, straight across the muddy patch and into a half-built house.

There were no workmen in, because of the weather. But by the time they reached the gap Bernard had a fair idea that they were beaten. Sure enough, as Shofiq pulled open the split-wood fence, Dougie said it.

'Eh up, Shofiq! We can't go in there! Not in ruddy weather like this!'

'Weather!' said Shofiq. He looked right comical, covered in half an inch of snow over a thin sports jacket thing he had on over his green jumper. It was amazing, how he could stand the cold.

Terry said nervously: 'It's hell's muddy, Shofiq. We've all got us best coats on. Us mums'd kill us.'

Even Maureen was silent. Bernard got the message; he'd known it all along.

'Let 'em go, Shofiq,' he said. 'It's dark, and it's nearly their bedtime. Go on, Maureen,' he added nastily. 'Nice man on telly'll tell you a Jackanory story.'

'It's all very well for you, Bernard Kershaw,' she said. 'You don't have to wear a daft coat when it's snowing. Remember that policeman in school, though. And look at that mud. Let's wait another time.'

'Talking of police,' said Shofiq. 'There's one of 'em now. Look, by the supermarket. We'd best scarper.'

They didn't need a second telling. Bernard was with them, or would have been, but as they flew off down the hill Shofiq grabbed his anorak hood and nearly choked him.

'Eh up, lad!' he said. 'Not you too!'

'What do you mean?' gasped Bernard. 'The copper!'

'In this weather? I can't even see supermarket, duck-egg, let alone a bobby. I just wanted rid. Come on, let's get in.'

'What?' said Bernard. 'On us own, like?'

Shofiq grinned.

'Come on,' he said. 'We'll give 'em a battering they'll never forget.'

They stood staring at each other, and Bernard knew he would have to go. Shofiq's eyes were blazing, and his father's lessons were bright in his own mind. But by the 'eck – he felt . . . he felt . . .

He crushed *any* thoughts, and dived for the gap, almost pushing Shofiq to one side.

'Right lad, you're on!' he said. 'Just give me first bash, that's all!'

# Chapter Twelve

BERNARD did get first bash, in a manner of speaking. As he dived for the hole a heavy hand got the side of his head from behind, and a voice said: 'Get out of it, our Bernard, before I belt your backside.' It was his sister Wendy.

Shofiq jumped like a scalded cat and was about to run off. But Wendy gave him a smile and said: 'Hang about, lad, hang about. I won't eat you. Now, our kid, what's all this then? Where the hell d'you think you're going?'

The two boys stood in front of Wendy looking at the slushy pavement. She was in her school coat, which was thick with snow, and she had a fluffy wool hat on her head that made it look like a great big football, only white. She poked Bernard in the ribs.

'Come on, lad, out with it. You were going to do the buildings, weren't you? In this weather, too. You're puddled. You're a right dumpling, you are.'

'No we weren't, our Wendy,' said Bernard. 'We were just looking, that's all. We saw some kids go in.'

'Ha ruddy ha,' she said. 'And look at the state of you, too. You're covered in snow. You're soaked to ruddy skin. You'll both get your death of cold! Who's this, anyway?'

'That's my mate,' said Bernard. 'He's called Shofiq. He's a Pakistani.'

Wendy laughed.

'Thanks very much, I'm sure,' she said. 'I wouldn't have known if you hadn't mentioned it.' She turned to Shofiq.

'I don't know why you bother with him, lad,' she said. 'He's a proper fool. You'd have thought he'd have noticed you sort of stand out against the snow, wouldn't you!'

Bernard was shocked. He hoped Shofiq wouldn't get miffed about that sort of talk. But Shofiq fell about.

'Aye,' he replied. 'They reckon folk in Blackburn are right glad about it – it makes us easier to pick out for shooting!'

'Any road,' said Wendy. 'Get out of that, our Bern, and come home. The last thing I want is for you to get pneumonia. That'd just about put the tin lid on it.'

Bernard felt bad. He looked helplessly at Shofiq, who'd have to go off all alone. No fight, no fun, not even a cup of tea.

'As for you,' said Wendy, 'you must be as daft as my brother. Look at the state of you in that summer jacket. I reckon I'll have to lend you a nightie!'

Bernard was scandalised, ashamed at the rudeness of it. Again Shofiq laughed.

'I'm all right, ta,' he said. 'I'll nip off home, like. I'll soon be warm.'

'You will heck,' said Wendy. 'You'll come with me and our Bernard, and no argument. You'll have a cup of tea and a rub-down and you'll wait till this blizzard gives over.' She poked Bernard again. 'Off; come on. Get ruddy moving, lad, sharpish.'

Bernard could hardly credit it.

'But what if me dad comes . . . ?'

'Well what if he does?' asked Wendy, pushing him along before her up the hill. 'He's not going to do owt, is he? What d'you think, lad? Just shut up and walk.'

Inside the flat Bernard was still half in a daze. He'd never really believed Shofiq would ever be able to see the inside of it, just as he never expected to be let inside his house. Although they were mates, and it would normally be one of the first things that happened, to prove they liked each other, sort of, he knew – he felt – that there were barriers. It had been weird enough him and Shofiq getting to be pals, at first, then weird the way he'd got him in the gang. But with grown-ups. Well, it had just seemed impossible. They had such funny ideas; they seemed to get on with so few folk, to sort of hate most of 'em.

His mum had been sitting in her easy chair in the kitchen when they came in, asleep with her legs splayed out and her mouth wide open. She was very pale, with great black bags of loose skin under her eyes, sort of snoring, a wet, bubbly sound. Bernard wanted to keep her hidden, to make sure Shofiq didn't see her, because he was ashamed, deadly ashamed. But their Wendy didn't seem to mind. She went up to mum and shook her gently, smiling at the boys over her shoulder.

'Put the kettle on, Bern, then the both of you take everything wet off. This is our mum, Shofiq. She's not been right well so she's not looking her best. You won't mind that, will you?'

Shofiq shook his head. He was staring.

'Give us your anorak, Bernard,' he said. 'I'll shake off snow outside front door. Shall I do yours . . . ?'

'Wendy,' said Wendy. 'Yeah, good idea. Thanks, lad.'

Mum, when she awoke, which took some little time because of the pills, was very vague and dozy. She smiled at Shofiq, though, and said how nice it was to see Bernard with a little friend in. She didn't even notice, as far as Bernard could tell, that he was a Pakistani. Still, she was dozy, there was no doubt about it. She was always dozy, on account of those pills. She hadn't even opened the paper today, not even upside down.

Wendy made tea, and made Bernard take off his jeans and put on some fresh. Shofiq was soaked to the skin, his green jumper and his black jeans. She took his coat off of him and hung it over one of the radiator things – the flat was heated automatically, whether you liked it or not – but she didn't press him about anything else. She'd said:

'Well just your jersey then,' but he'd shaken his head shyly. Bernard guessed he had a dirty vest on, or maybe nothing at all. He was funny about clothes, was Shofiq. He didn't appear to feel the cold and he always wore the same, always. It was a mystery.

They had quite a nice time, one way and another, messing about for a while while Wendy cooked tea and mum sat in front of the telly, watching the kids' programmes, but as it got later and later, Bernard got more and more tense. His dad sometimes came home very early these days, because of short-time working and that, and you could never tell. He kept glancing hopefully at the weather out of the window, but it was snowing hard and the wind was battering against the flats like mad. He got tenser and tenser.

At last the moment he'd been dreading arrived. He was as taut as a bowstring, and jumped when the key went in the front door lock. He turned to Shofiq and whispered: 'Here's me dad. Ee. Ruddy hell.'

They stayed in the bedroom for a while longer, but somehow Bernard was drawn to the living room where his dad would be. He didn't want to see him, didn't want him to see Shofiq, didn't know how he'd react to him being mates with a 'fog inspector'. But there was nothing he could do about it. He lost interest in their game, he got jumpier and jumpier. In the end he said: 'Come on then, lad. We'd best go and say "How do" to the old feller.'

Dad was sitting slopped out in an armchair with his legs stuck out and his dirty boots on the mat. He was in overalls, with his reading glasses, funny old wire ones, stuck on the end of his nose, reading the paper. A mug of tea was balanced on the arm of the chair.

Bernard entered the room first, and Dad looked up with a tired smile.

'Hello, lad. Had a good day? Ruddy awful weather out there . . .'

He stopped. Shofiq had appeared. His dad pushed his glasses further down his nose with a frown, looking over them.

'Oh, sorry,' he said. 'Didn't know you had a mate in. Who's this then?'

It was daft; simple. It was just as if his dad had never come out with all those tales from the mill, just as if he'd never been heard to say 'I hate Pakis, me' in his life. Bernard felt an utter drip, he'd been so feared. Wendy came in with the teapot and laughed.

'Don't look such a gawp, our Bern. I told you nobody was going to get ate, didn't I?'

Shofiq refused to eat any tea, but Wendy still reckoned he couldn't go home, and her dad agreed. It was a proper blizzard, he said, the worst so far. It'd probably thaw, it usually did pretty quick these days, but at the moment it was very bad. Shofiq sat to one side, glancing at a comic, while the family had their food.

Bernard's mum started the conversation that made things bad. She'd sat for some time, picking at her plate, hardly eating anything as usual, and saying the odd thing every now and again. Dad usually only gave a grunt, because most of what she said wasn't all that particular, didn't call for real answers. Then she said: 'How's it at the mill, dear? Have you sacked all them fellers yet?'

'Oh not all that again,' said Wendy quickly. She probably said it because she saw what might be coming, Bernard guessed. But she'd said the wrong thing.

'What's up with you then, our Wendy?' said her father. 'Not interested in anyone's ruddy future but your own, eh? You're just all ruddy self, girl, that's your trouble. You never think of no one, but Number One – Miss Wendy Ruddy Kershaw.'

Wendy went that odd colour she went when she was riled. Because of her red hair and pale skin she could go a right queer shade.

'It's not a case of that, our dad,' she said hotly. 'You

107

know rotten well I care about other people's futures. I'm just not so sure that . . .'

She tailed off.

'That what?' asked her father grimly. 'Go on, lass, spit it out. That what?'

Wendy stuck her face down doggedly and put a big forkful of food in her mouth. She chewed it hard, determined not to speak. Her father stared at her for some time; you could see his anger fading. He took a mouthful of tea, then went on more quietly :

'The redundancies are definite. About eighty jobs have got to go, and they've got to go fast. What d'you want me to do? Give myself the sack? Volunteer? We'd all starve, Miss, and *you're* not much help on that score.'

Wendy chewed silently on. Bernard's mum smiled vaguely at Shofiq and said : 'Mr Kershaw's in the textiles, dear. Down the mill. They have a lot of problems.'

'Now now, love,' said his dad warningly. 'The lad don't want to hear all this.'

'Oh well, he might,' said Bernard's mum with a smile. 'A lot of Pakis work in the mills, you know.'

Bernard watched in amazement as his father slowly blushed brick red. Shofiq tried to help out the embarrassment. He was still cool and calm, he was a ruddy marvel. But he, like Wendy and Bernard's mum, managed to say the wrong thing.

'My dad is in textiles as it happens, Mr Kershaw,' he said. 'He works at Regal.'

'He used to be a skilled man back in India,' said Bernard, proud for his friend. 'But now he can only get a job as . . .'

He stopped, his mouth gaping. Wendy's mouth was gaping too, and his father's colour had gone from red to even redder. Regal! That's where *his* dad worked!

'Well,' said his father at last. 'Well I'm sorry, lad, I really am. I wish nothing had been said, and we'd best forget all about it. It's not table talk any road, and it's not for the likes of kids to be discussing. It's serious matters, it's business, and it's men's work.'

'Oh yes,' said Wendy furiously. She just couldn't stop herself, you could tell. 'You just don't want anyone to know how you and your honest union chums organise it so's people who've been good workers for years are going to get the push just because of the colour of their skin, that's all. That's what he means, Shofiq lad, no danger.'

Bernard's father looked at Wendy as if he'd kill her. He was panting.

'You're going to get a beating for that, my girl,' he said. 'I'd leave the room if I were you. I'd leave bloody house and never come back.'

Wendy was dead white, just her freckles glaring out like orange splodges. Dad turned to Shofiq. Bernard was shaking now, even his mother was beginning to realise there was something going on. But Shofiq was calm. He raised his eyes politely to Dad's, and they were unafraid.

He said: 'I better be going, Mr Kershaw. It'll have stopped snowing by now, I reckon.'

Mr Kershaw shook his head.

'Now listen, lad. It's not like you think. Honestly, our Wendy's a right little monkey sometimes. It's her red hair. She's wild. I don't know. But it's not our fault, this sacking do, it's not my fault. We have a lot of trouble with the Pakistanis, if you'll let me be frank, they're more trouble than soft Mick, some of 'em. They're always stopping working for religion, some festival do or summat, they're always getting out their mats and that for a quick pray, they won't use the canteen, they make no bloody effort. It's a fact, lad, it can't be denied. If they'd change, fair enough. If they'd try to do it our way, all right. But they won't, they don't. It's a problem.'

There was a pause. Then Shofiq said: 'You'd like to see us integrate?'

Bernard's father beamed.

'That's it!' he said. '*You* understand, see. Integrate,

that's the word. Ruddy hell, lad, you even talk the language like one of us. You've got a thicker accent than our Bern there. Some of the men *we* work with can't hardly talk the – '

'Dad!'

It was Bernard. It was almost a shriek. Shofiq smiled. There was an awkward pause.

Wendy said bitterly: 'Last in first out's the rule. Are you telling me the white men who started work *after* the Asians'll get the sack first, eh?'

Her dad said tiredly: 'Wendy, shut your mouth and leave, lass. I won't belt you, even if you do deserve it. You mean well, lass, but shut your mouth, please. You don't know the half of it.' He said to Shofiq: 'It's nothing personal, lad, nothing personal, and it's not like that at all. We've got to protect our own. You immigrants – you're good people, I'm sure; I mean, there's good and bad everywhere, but . . . well, you know.'

'Aye, I do, Mr Kershaw,' said Shofiq quietly. 'I think I know, anyway. But I'm not actually an immigrant, in actual fact. I were born here, like. My dad – I don't think *he* understands, that's all.'

There was another long pause. Bernard's mother was looking very ill. The black patches under her eyes were huge.

'And my mum,' said Shofiq, very very quietly. 'I'm sure she doesn't. It's a problem. She just doesn't understand.'

After a time Wendy said: 'It's stopped snowing. Get your things on, Bernard, you can see Shofiq home, it's a nice night for a walk, clear your lungs out. I'm going to get our mum to bed.'

She added: 'You can give us a hand, Dad, or go and have a pint, cheer yourself up. You look as if you need it. I've got a lot of homework to do after washing dishes.'

Nobody argued. Five minutes later Bernard and Shofiq were well down the hill.

It was, in fact, a beautiful night. Even the dirty sort of town was clean and bright, with hardly any traffic moving except on the main roads, which the boys kept well clear of. The snow was thick, they reckoned about four inches, and soft and fluffy. The wind had died right away to nothing, and they took great lungfuls of air and blasted them out into the night as steam. The sky was vast and cloudless, with millions and billions and trillions of stars winking at them. In spite of themselves they felt better. They relaxed. The misery of the awful scene in the house dwindled slowly away.

By the time they'd reached the last couple of streets before Cardigan Road, where Shofiq lived, they'd got to talking like proper mates again, saying things they wouldn't say to anyone else, or sometimes wouldn't like to admit even to themselves, alone. They were talking over what had happened in Bernard's flat, when Shofiq said something that floored him completely.

'Your mum looks dead ill, Bernard,' he said. 'I were proper sick about that. I reckon she must have the same as my mum's got. She looks just like her, just exactly like her.'

Bernard could have shrieked, he was so stunned. His mother – like Shofiq's! But, but – but Shofiq's mum was mad! Oh my God, surely he couldn't mean it? His mum was ill, that's all, since the baby thing. But Shofiq's mum . . . Could it be that . . . ?

At that moment they turned the corner from one of the little alleyways into Cardigan Road. Standing in front of Shofiq's house was something that filled Bernard with dread, then with a sudden shock of relief.

'Oh crikey!' said Shofiq. 'Oh no, oh crikey, no!'

He started to run.

'No, Bernard!' he shouted, as Bernard made to go too. 'No, please, please no! Go! Leave me be, go home, go!'

Bernard stopped, his mind a jumble of confused thoughts. If this had happened it couldn't be the same!

His mum couldn't be like Shofiq's! But what *had* happened? And what would the poor lad do now?

He watched for a little while, till someone on a stretcher had been carried from the house and put into the ambulance, but he watched from the dark corner of the alley. He felt ashamed, as if he was spying, doing something rotten to his friend.

When the ambulance had gone he walked slowly home, not worried at all, these days, about being alone down the Brook. He was sad, and happy, and confused. It was terrible. But at least his mum couldn't be ill like Shofiq's. No, no danger.

# Chapter Thirteen

THE snow, as his dad had predicted, didn't last long. Bernard raced to school as fast as he possibly could, not caring that he got his legs soaked up to the knees and beyond in the freezing, slushy puddles. He had a quick glance around the Jericho croft, not bothering to be a spy, but there was no sign of Shofiq. He couldn't see him in assembly either, and ten minutes after classes began he had to admit that he wasn't coming in.

At playtime, and after dinner, the gang met to talk about this and that. They wanted to know what had happened after Shofiq had seen the cop the night before, and where he and Bernard had got to. Bernard explained that there hadn't been one, and was inclined to give them a rubbishing for not wanting to go in the buildings and fight anyway. But he knew they'd been right – or at least not very wrong – about the weather, and the vandal-warning and that. There'd be another time, and it wasn't worth falling out over. Anyway, he was much more anxious about his mate. He explained that Wendy had nabbed them, and he said Shofiq had come to his place, where they'd played for a while and had a cup of tea. But he didn't let out much more.

By dinnertime next day, Maureen knew more about why Shofiq wasn't there than Bernard. It was the talk of the Glossop Street canteen, where her mum worked, and it was a real odd do. Bernard listened in silence while she rattled on about Shofiq's mum being hauled off to St

James's, nutty as a fruitcake, raving she was. The baby had been taken too, to be looked after by nurses. It was a terrible thing, said Maureen, the poor little baby. Apparently Shofiq and his dad had wanted to keep it, to look after it themselves, but that was barmy, men couldn't do with babies! And his sister, what got bussed, had been brought to Glossop Street by a man in a car, she reckoned it was the one they'd seen that night, the pale blue Cortina, but she'd run off at playtime.

'She never cried, though,' put in Dougie. 'Never even looked like it. A real cool'un.'

'Hard,' said Maureen. 'A real little hard piece, my mum says. She's never cried, never. She don't speak, nor do nothing. She needs to go in care, my mum says.'

Bernard didn't argue, or ask how the heck the dinner ladies knew, or fight back, although he was certain all this was wrong, that it shouldn't be happening, and that he shouldn't let them talk about Shofiq's family like this. But he didn't know how to defend them, what to say or do for the best. He wanted to see Shofiq, to talk, to find out. He missed him.

Even then, though, he was afraid. He still hadn't got over what Shofiq had said. He'd looked at his own mum in a different way, and got worried sick. She *wasn't* well, she *wasn't* right. Those pills seemed to make her like a kind of doll, as if she wasn't properly alive. He'd asked Wendy about it, but she'd not said much. She'd said his mum had had a bad do, losing the baby and that, and she was depressed. She'd said she'd get better. Bernard hadn't dared to ask the question he really wanted to ask: Is my mum mad? He couldn't ask it, or even the other, easier question: Could people *reckon* she was mad? He told himself that Wendy would have laughed at him for asking, that was all. But he wasn't fooling himself. He just didn't have the guts to ask, in case of what the answers might be.

Maureen and Terry and Dougie tried to get his mind off

Shofiq, but their lack of worry about him made Bernard angry. To them it was just a thing, just something to chat about. He avoided them as much as possible, even when they sought him out at the end of playtime with some bad news. They practically had to corner him to tell him that Bobby Whitehead was after their blood.

'It's dead serious, Bern,' said Terry. 'He's got it all tied up with Sammy Woods and Peter Winterbottom I reckon. It won't be long now, he said, and he said you ought to know about it. I thought he were going to thump me, but he just wanted to gloat. He said to tell you it was your last warning.'

'Us chasing him into the buildings didn't help,' said Maureen. 'Judith Wintle says him and Pat Broome got into a terrible row over that. Their clothes were ruinated. She lives in same block as Pat,' she added.

Bernard sighed.

'Stands to reason he'll try and do us now,' he said. 'Now we've lost Shofiq for a while. Stands to reason.' But he still couldn't summon up much interest in it, and he got into the classroom as fast as he could, to be on his own.

After school, fed up to the back teeth, Bernard shook off the gang by saying he had to get some errands, and set off down the Brook. When he started, he wasn't sure he was going there, but his feet led the way. The snow and slush were all gone, but it was still very cold, with a fine, soaking drizzle. He didn't have the foggiest idea of what he'd do when he arrived, but he had to find out what was going on. Shofiq's two little sisters had come to school that morning, although they'd taken off the day after the ambulance do, but he'd got no sense out of them at all, although they knew him and weren't afraid. They'd just gone all shy and looked at the ground, and muttered under their breath.

One of the reasons he decided to go, was that the school was off next day, to be used as an election place. The gang were chuffed about having a buckshee day off, and wanted to plan something. He found himself walking down the Brook because he didn't want to even have a day off without Shofiq. He was miserable. He wanted to know. He missed his mate.

It was more or less dark when he got to Number 27 Cardigan Road. It was a dingy old door, that had once been bright yellow and black, but was now a dull, dirty colour. He stood on tiptoe to ring the bell, but because he couldn't hear it buzzing inside he knocked as well, quite hard. Then he listened at the letter-box.

He heard noises, voices, then they stopped. He banged again, feeling a right duck-egg, then looked through the letter-box. He thought he saw someone move, in the darkness at the end of the passage. But there was no more sound.

All right, thought Bernard savagely. If that's the way you want it, Shofiq Rahman. He thought vaguely of blowing off the lock with his Luger, but only for a second. He hadn't bothered much with Lugers, or spying, or whatnot lately. Too much important was happening, that pretend pistols were no help at all with, no help at all.

He started to walk away, then stopped. He stood on the edge of the pavement, just stood there, outside the house, for a long time. Then he sat down, plonk, on the kerb, and felt the cold water from the stones soak through the seat of his jeans, and through his pants. He put his chin in his hands and began to shiver. Tears came to his eyes, but even he didn't know if he was crying or not. Maybe it was just the rotten cold, and the drizzle, and the damp.

He hardly heard the faint click when the door opened at last. Shofiq's voice said quietly : 'You'd best come in, Bern. You'll catch your death out there. You're a stubborn get, you are.'

Bernard was so cold, and miserable, that the fact of actually doing what he never thought he would – get inside Shofiq's house – didn't sink in. He gave Shofiq a wan smile, which Shofiq returned with an even less happy one, and followed him down the passage.

'I wanted to see you, lad,' he said. 'I've been right worried.'

'Aye,' said Shofiq. 'You'd best come in here.'

They went into a room off the passage that had a big old-fashioned gas-fire in it. The two little sisters were sitting in an armchair, side by side, holding hands and watching a portable telly. The other sister, the queer one, was sitting at the end of a sofa, that matched the arm-chair. She didn't look up when the boys came in. She had her hands in her lap, but her fingers weren't moving.

'Park yourself in front of the fire and have a warm,' said Shofiq. 'Stick your bottom out, lad, try and get it dry. Your sister'll half kill you.'

None of the others spoke. Bernard put his back to the fire and began to steam. Shofiq offered him a cup of tea but he refused. The telly droned on. Shofiq sat down on the sofa and closed his eyes. For a while Bernard just stood there, feeling the heat going through him. He looked at the room.

Apart from the smell, and some sort of coloured silky cloths lying around, it could have been anyone's house. In fact, it reminded him quite strongly of his old Auntie Violet's terrace on the other side of town, before it was pulled down and she and Uncle Wally had died. It had the big settee, and the two big armchairs, and a faded and worn old carpet, like a lot of old houses. There were two pictures on the wall, one of a huge deer thing, with horns, and one of a gang of white horses on a sea shore, just like his Auntie Mary and Uncle Jeff had on their wall; the same picture by the look of it, which was funny: he'd thought artists only did one. On the wall opposite, straight in front of him, was a little motto thing, done out with a red-hot poker on wood. It said: 'Today is the tomorrow we worried about yesterday but all is well'. He gave up trying to work that out after ten seconds. Gibberish.

He wasn't disappointed that the house wasn't different,

or weird, or strange. In a way he was glad. It smelled, no doubt about that, it smelled like Shofiq did: of curry, and cooking and things, but that was that. It was a nice smell, once you'd got used to it. He liked to smell Shofiq, now, when they were having a friendly wrestle; he knew the smell – it was his mate. So the house was the same as anyone else's. He should've known.

Shofiq was fidgetting. When he thought about it, Bernard could tell he wanted him gone. He blushed, then crushed his embarrassment. Ruddy hell, he'd made a right berk of himself to get himself let in: no point in warming his bum up and pushing off now, was there? But what could he say?

All sorts of questions flitted through his head, but he couldn't ask any of them, could he? Like: 'Where's your dad, then?' Or: 'Is it true your mum's been took off to hospital, to St James's?' Or: 'What's happened to baby boy, have the council took him off you?' So in the end he said: 'How's it been then? Long time no see.'

Shofiq looked at his face and it was Bernard who looked away. He recognised his friend's courage and it made him feel good. If only he could know what was going on in his head, though; he'd often wished that. He pulled his eyes back to Shofiq's and held them there. If Shofiq could look him in the eye with the trouble he was in, then he could hold his own too. By the heck, though, Shofiq looked miserable. He looked pig sick.

'Why don't you come out and play tomorrow,' he said. 'It'd do you good. Daft to be stuck inside all day. We've got it off from school. For election day, you know.'

It was a daft thing to say, and he knew it. Some hopes of Shofiq being able to come for a lark. Shofiq managed to show him a little smile, though.

'Thanks, pal. But I can't. I've to go to Social Security offices in town.'

'Hey, great!' said Bernard. 'Are you going to burn 'em down? Can I come?'

118

Shofiq actually laughed.

'You're a right fool you are, Bernard,' he said. 'By hell though, I've a mind to at that! A gallon of petrol and some matches . . .' His smile faded. 'You better go now, Bernard. Would you mind?'

'Well look though,' said Bernard quickly. 'I mean, can I come too? I mean, I've nowt else to do, you know. I'll come with you.'

'No,' said Shofiq sharply. 'No, it's not like that. It's business. I've got to sort things out.'

'But I'm your mate!' said Bernard. 'I'm your pal! I'll come with you, give you a hand. I'd like to.'

Shofiq moved his head from side to side. He looked hunted.

'Look, Bern, I know you're me mate and that. But – heck, lad, leave us be! I'll have to ask you to go. There's someone due. Oh Bernard, leave me be!'

His eyes were swimming with tears. Bernard felt his own filling. Heck, heck, this was awful.

Suddenly there was a loud knock at the door. Shofiq, Bernard, and the two little girls jumped as if they'd been shot. Only the big sister didn't move. She was quite still, staring straight at the gas-fire. Shofiq grabbed Bernard's arm. His eyes were quite wild, and he began to babble.

'Say . . . tell him . . . say . . . Bernard, will you tell this feller . . .' He broke off, then jabbered at the two little girls in that foreign language. One of them started to cry, but tried to stop when he jabbered again. Then he went up to the queer girl, and touched her shoulder, and spoke to her, quiet, in the same language. The knocker went again, hard, frightening.

'Bern,' he said. 'You're my mate, right? Tell this feller me dad's just gone out if he asks, right? Say you're here for a while. All right?'

'Who is it? Is it that social worker berk?'

'Just follow what I say, Bernard. Please.' Shofiq disappeared. Bernard looked round the room, flustered.

Blinking heck, this was something! He hadn't bargained on this, no mistake!

It was the social worker. He came in with his daft Russian hat in his mitt, wearing the furry sheepskin and a friendly-looking smile. Friendly and a little grim. He looked right astonished when he saw Bernard.

Shofiq said: 'Would you like to sit down, sir? This is Bernard Kershaw, my friend who's come to help me baby-sit. Bernard, this is Mr Burke from the Social Services. He helps us out, like, helps out the family.'

Bernard blushed crimson.

'Pleased to meet you, mister,' he said.

Mr Burke smiled.

'Hello, lad,' he said.

You smarmy little get, Bernard thought. I'd like to smash you.

Shofiq's sister stood up from the end of the settee. Her face was like a rock, and a strange, grey, chalky colour.

'I get tea for you.'

'No no!' said Mr Burke. 'I've just come to have a few words with your daddy. Sit down, my dear, I don't want tea.'

She walked past him without looking at him. Her pyjama things rustled softly.

'Tea,' she said. 'I get tea for you.'

When she'd gone Shofiq said: 'She's still sort of upset, sir. She'll be all right. When Mum and the baby . . . well, you know. Please sit down, sir, please.'

'Well,' said Mr Burke. 'It's your dad I came to see really. Listen, lad, tell her not to bother with the tea. Really, I'm quite all right.'

Shofiq gave a little sort of bow. Without moving he said something foreign towards the half-open door. There was no reply.

'That will be all right, sir,' he said. 'She hears me. But I'm afraid you've missed my father. He's out arranging a sitter.'

That shook Bernard. I thought I were meant to be the sitter, he thought. He listened hard. Even if Shofiq changed the plan, *he* wouldn't let him down. He'd follow all right.

'Oh dear,' said Mr Burke. 'That's a pity. How do you mean though, a sitter? Will he be long?'

'I can't rightly say, sir,' said Shofiq. 'He's gone to find a neighbour or a friend to come and look after us kids. While he goes to hospital to see our mum, sir. I expect he'll be . . . half an hour. Maybe more.'

'So you children are alone? There's no one looking after you?'

Shofiq gave a small, polite smile.

'Well, that's so I suppose,' he said. 'But I mean, there is me here, and my mate Bernard. We're hardly babies, sir. We're both quite capable of cooking a kettle or calling fire brigade if the house burns down.'

Bernard, greatly daring, said: 'It won't be long, sir. Mr Rahman said half an hour, sir. I said I'd stay on. To help, like.'

'My father must see my mother, sir. That's absolutely necessary, isn't it?'

Mr Burke looked at his watch. He bit his lip. He played with his daft Russian fur hat for a minute or two. He sucked his teeth, making a clicking noise with his top lip.

'Listen,' he said at last. 'I'm going to trust you, Ahmed. I know you're a good boy, a bright boy. If you promise me, absolutely promise me on your honour, that your father will be back soon, and will provide a sitter if he goes to the hospital, I'll . . . I'll leave it at that.' He gave a big winning smile. 'Is it a deal?' he said, in a jolly tone.

Shofiq smiled gravely.

'Yes, sir,' he said. 'Of course. He may be even less than half an hour, if you want to wait.'

'No no,' said Mr Burke. 'That will be all right. It was

not too important. I can see him another day, can't I?
If he needs me.'

'Of course, sir,' replied Shofiq. 'You're always welcome,
sir, right welcome.'

'Well done!' said Mr Burke. 'Good man, Ahmed!'

He narrowed his eyes.

'Now listen, old lad,' he went on. 'Seriously and man
to man : you're a bright fellow. You do *understand*, don't
you, that I'm only here to help? I want to make life
easier for you, you know that, don't you? Things can be
hard, Mummy ill and Daddy having to work. We wouldn't
want to see the little ones suffer, now would we?'

'No, sir,' said Shofiq. 'Of course not.'

'So if anything goes wro . . . if anything crops up,
anything at all . . . you know what to do for the best?'

Shofiq pointed to a plaster statue on the mantelpiece.

'I have your telephone number under there, Mr Burke,'
he said. 'I have three numbers. Century House, Gateway
House and your home. It's right . . . it's extremely kind
of you, sir.'

The social worker fellow looked dead chuffed. Bernard
was inwardly goggling. What a cool one, this Shofiq! He
were ruddy brilliant!

When the man had gone, Shofiq showed a different
side, just for a few seconds. He leaned against a wall with
his eyes tight shut. His face had gone greyish-brown,
something like his funny sister's. Bernard wanted to ask
where his father really was, what was going on, what
was going to happen. But he didn't. He knew he had to
leave Shofiq alone, and fast.

To make sure Mr Burke couldn't possibly see him, to
show you didn't forget your Secret Service training easy,
he left through the back kitchen. He said tarah to
Shofiq, and he said he'd see him next day. Shofiq said not
a word, which Bernard took to mean he hadn't said no.

He belted across the park at a rate of knots, keeping a
weather eye open for dirty old men. When he got to

Gateway House, dark and apparently deserted for the night, he stood and studied it for a while.

It'd be a piece of cake to burn that down, a piece of cake. It didn't even have a proper wall round it.

He put his head down and ran to his tea.

# Chapter Fourteen

BERNARD was afraid he was going to have missed Shofiq next day, because as he had it off, Wendy had organised him to do all sorts of extra things. He argued for a while, saying he had something dead important to do, but he got nowhere. In Wendy's book, if you had some spare time you had to pull your weight in it. As it happened, he got down the Brook at just the right moment. He turned the corner into Cardigan Road at the very second Shofiq was closing the front door. What was more, because he'd been working around the flat all morning, Bernard had managed to nick a box of matches, in case they decided to burn down the social workers' offices.

Shofiq didn't look exactly pleased to see him, but he managed a smile. Bernard tried to pump him on their walk into the town centre, but Shofiq said practically nothing. It was a cold day again, but dry, and they walked along side by side, pretty morose, with the breath blowing round their heads.

The centre of town was always busy, and Bernard avoided it as much as he could. But Shofiq seemed to know his way about all right; he didn't have to ask directions or anything. When they got to Century House Bernard would have walked past, never dreaming that the place they were after could be so huge. When Shofiq led him through the wide glass doors into the lobby he was amazed. The carpet was about a foot thick, and there were big ornaments, and lifts, and an information desk the size of their best room. Behind it were lots of old fellows in sort of soldiers' clothes, with flat hats and medals. Bernard was sweating cobs, but Shofiq didn't even glance at them. He marched over to a lift and pressed a button.

A couple of minutes later there was a faint 'ding' and the doors slid open. He pushed Bernard in and pressed another button. The doors closed and they went up to the second floor. Bernard was still speechless. The lift was so different from the ones in the flats that he didn't know where to turn. No smell, no pictures or slogans scratched on the sides – and it worked.

The place they came out into was a large hall affair. All along one side of it was glass, with little windows in it like in the post office, with girls and blokes sat on chairs behind them. Each window had only one or two people standing on the other side, the public side, but Bernard soon worked out why. Instead of standing up to queue, everyone sat down. The main part of the hall was all black plastic chairs, with dozens and dozens of people sat on them.

'What *is* it?' he whispered.

'It's the Social Security,' Shofiq replied. 'You know. The dole, unemployment, the sick pay, all that sort of stuff.'

'What, all these people are here because they're sick or summat?'

'Something like that,' said Shofiq. 'Just belt up a minute till I find the right window.'

It dawned on Bernard after a while that this was where the scroungers came. His dad was always on about the scroungers. Apparently, half the population of England was on the scrounge. They never did no work and they had dozens of kids, and decent folk kept 'em by paying taxes. Most of them, according to his dad, were Pakistanis, or West Indians, or Irish. He looked around. There did seem to be a lot of Pakistanis, and there were one or two real coal-black faces, with frizzy hair. But there were a lot of white people, too. How could you tell if they were Irish, he wondered. It was a problem.

Shofiq more or less pushed him around like a sheep till he found the little window he wanted. How he knew it was the right one, Bernard didn't even try to guess, but they sat at the end of a row and set out to wait their turn. He looked right sick about it, too, when he saw the girl he had to speak to. He looked so sick, in fact, that Bernard whispered: 'What's up, then? D'you recognise her?'

'Aye,' said Shofiq. 'Just keep your fingers crossed, that's all. If she's had a bad day we'll get some stick, no danger. She can be a right terror.'

Bernard stared, interested. She looked quite fit to him. Dead pretty if he had to be honest. She didn't look like no ogre, that was certain. Shofiq saw him staring. He gave a little smile.

'You can never tell by looking, lad,' he said. 'You just take my word for it. Some of 'em here look horrible and they're right nice, it's dead funny. That lass you can't trust. If she's had a good easy day she's champion, couldn't be better. But if she's been bashing her head against a brick wall, like, she gets right nowty. Knackered, you know. It makes her bad-tempered.'

'Do you know her then?' Bernard asked. 'Do you see her a lot?'

'Nah,' said Shofiq. 'Not a lot. She used to be over there, on the sick counter. I used to come about me mum. She gets . . . she gets *frustrated*, knackered. You can't trust her.'

'That's daft that,' said Bernard. 'I mean, how can you get knackered in an office, eh? I mean, you don't even do no ruddy work to speak of. They're all lazy so and so's in offices, my dad says. Bone idle sods.'

Shofiq didn't reply. He just shook his head, as if to say there was more to it all than Bernard would understand. Bernard might have been upset by this, but he had a vague feeling he was lost anyway. He thought of scroungers again, and all the stuff his dad had told him.

Even the row they were sitting on added to his confusion, because although most of the people were Pakistanis, right in the middle there was an English woman, with two little kids. She wasn't Irish neither, because her accent was dead local. The kids were pale, and manky-looking, and their mum wasn't much better. She looked like she'd just come out of hospital, where they'd taken out all her insides and chucked 'em in the bin. White as a ghost, only dirtier.

The waiting went on and on, it nearly drove him barmy. Worst of all, Shofiq didn't want to talk. He wouldn't talk, in fact. He just sat there, looking grim. He smiled once, just once, when Bernard called him Ahmed, like the social worker fellow had done. But it was a right nasty smile at that.

In the end they were only two from the window. The white woman had gone, taking her two manky brats as well. They had to leave a gap where they should have sat, because one of the kids had wet itself on the plastic seat. It had occurred to Bernard, not long after that, that it was a ruddy funny way to get your money, this scrounging. He'd sooner have a job any day. He felt Shofiq getting tense next to him, and he dragged his eyes down off a daft-looking picture on the wall, showing someone coughing after having a puff on a fag.

'What's up, lad?' he asked. 'Is it our turn?'

It wasn't. Shofiq was watching an old, bent Pakistani fellow, he looked about a hundred and fifty, trying to make himself understood at the little window. Bernard heard a note of anger in the voice of the smart-looking young lass behind the glass. She was getting right bad-tempered.

He couldn't quite catch what was going on, but it was odd to watch. The old man was thin, and very very small, with old blue trousers and a wrinkled coat made of plastic pretend leather. His face was dark brown, almost black, with a fringe of dead-white whiskers all round, on top and underneath. Something like a billygoat, he looked to Bernard, only his face was nice, like a good vicar in a picture, twinkly and friendly. But he also looked sad, very unhappy, and he kept making little movements with his hands, trying to make the girl understand. On top of his head he had a little cap affair, really small. And his feet had cracked shoes on; you could see his toes through one of them.

'What's going on, Shof?'

'Ssh!' went Shofiq. His face was angry. He couldn't speak properly.

'No,' Bernard heard the old man say. 'Yes. No. In England before zizz muzz.'

There was an angry noise behind the glass. The old man dropped some papers on the floor. He bent down for them very slowly. When he stood up again he peered into the glass. The smart-looking lass was waving her arms about.

Bernard just caught the words. She was more or less yelling. 'No use. Just no use at all. Fill in that form. The number is on the top left corner. Fill it in or I can't help. It's no use at all!'

She pushed another bit of paper out of her window and it shot off onto the floor. The old fellow bent slowly down and picked it up. He stood up again and said into the window: 'Plizz. I not know. I spike no . . .'

The girl waved her arms in front of her face as if she was frightening off a wasp.

'No!' she snapped. 'No use. Fill in that form and come back. FILL IT IN!'

The man stood there. He looked round helplessly. He lifted up the bunch of papers to the girl, then shook his head. He shuffled away towards the stairs. The girl stuck her face to the glass and called out: 'Next please. Come along now, we haven't got all day!'

The next man, a tall, good-looking Asian of about twenty in a smart suit, walked up to the window and pushed across a piece of paper. The girl looked at it, stamped it, gave it back. He walked off. Twenty seconds it had taken, at the most. Bernard shook his head in wonder. That feller had been sat there for nearly two hours.

'Is that it?' he said. 'Did that poor young . . .'

'Shut your gob and come on!' said Shofiq. 'She'll probably go for her tea break if we're not like greased lightning.'

Bernard crowded up behind Shofiq and stared in through the glass. She was a well turned-out lass, no doubt about that. Young, too, she couldn't have been above twentyish. She was pretty, but she had a nasty turn to her face, as though she didn't like folk much. He'd noticed that most of the people behind the windows were something like her, except for a couple who were older. They were mostly youngish, and wore dear-looking clothes, the blokes with wide ties on and pouffy hair-dos. It didn't seem right, somehow, that they should be dealing with all the poor folk in the hall. This lass, for instance: she were looking at them like something the cat had brought in.

'Well?' she said.

Bernard heard Shofiq swallow. He must be nervous. But his face was calm, his eyes wide open and intelligent. His voice was calm as well, and he'd put on his best accent.

'I wonder if you can help me please, miss?' he said. 'I'm calling on behalf of my father. I wish to find out all I can about a question of unfair dismissal. I also wish to enquire about the possibility of redundancy payments, and in general about unemployment benefits. My father is a textile worker, he is thirty-six years old next birthday, he has been in employment with the same company for near twelve years and he has five children. And a wife. Of course.'

The girl actually smiled. Not a very friendly smile, but she smiled.

'Very good,' she said. 'I can tell you, it's a real relief to find one of you lot that can speak the language! I suppose you were born here?'

'Yes, miss,' replied Shofiq.

'Live down the Brook?'

'Yes, miss.'

She made a 'humph' sound in her throat and pulled a pad of paper towards her.

'Right? What was all that again?'

Shofiq didn't bat an eyelid. Bernard was already beginning to smart. She was so *rude*. She was so ruddy rude. He swallowed noisily. Shofiq looked at him and scowled, warningly, as much as to say 'Keep your mouth shut!'

The girl said: 'If you're going to make funny faces all day, kindly do it elsewhere. I'm very busy.'

'I'm sorry, miss,' said Shofiq. 'What I wanted to know was...'

The girl made squiggles on the paper while he went through it all again, and a lot more. She didn't make proper notes though, because Bernard watched her. When Shofiq had finished she smiled.

'Well, that's that then,' she said. 'I can't help you, I'm afraid.'

Bernard's mouth dropped open.

'Why not, miss?' asked Shofiq.

'Well all this information obviously can't be given to a child. Utter waste of time. If your father wants it he will have to come himself.'

'But he can't, miss! He's got to work! And the kids!'

'Well, your mother then,' she said. 'Go on now, off you go. I'm very busy.'

'But me mum's in hospital! And I'm trying to *keep* his job, not have him...'

The girl smiled a proper icy smile this time.

'Don't you dare raise your voice to me, young fellow.

You've come to quite the wrong place for that question in any case. I can't help. Send your father in. I suppose he *can* read and write,' she added, crushingly.

'But he's got the sack! And me mum . . . me mum . . .'

'Please leave this window before I call a porter,' she snapped. 'You Pakis are all alike. If you think you can lay down the law to me . . .'

Shofiq turned away, his eyes bright. The girl looking at him with a proper smirk on her mug. Bernard looked full in her face.

'You bloody bitch,' he said. 'You manky, stuck-up, bloody cow.'

She said 'Oh!' in a shocked, disgusted way that anyone could see was put on. Then she shouted: 'Mr Simmons! Mr Simmons! These boys! Quickly!'

They didn't hang about to see what happened. They raced for the stairs and bounced down them two at a time. Bernard, by a bit of bad luck, knocked over a young girl, a girl of about sixteen, who was carrying a large tray of tea and biscuits. She fell down onto one knee and her glasses came off, and her tray went flying right over the banister. It was very spectacular, with the smashing of crockery and a monster brown stain that ran down the cream-painted wall of the stairs – it must have been coffee, not tea, after all.

Bernard, scared as he was, had to stop, because the girl was so upset. Her glasses hadn't broken – he picked them up and gave them to her – but she started to bawl. She was very young, not that older than his sister and much more like a kid than Wendy, who was dead smart, and he guessed it was probably her first job. Well that was all right; they wouldn't give her the sack because of a tray of coffee he'd knocked over. He stood there for a minute, wondering what the heck he could do. Which was nothing, he decided, so he went pelting off once more, shouting: 'Sorry, love! I didn't mean to knock you over!' as he ran.

On the next floor down he could see he was trapped. There were people streaming out of the doors at the top of the flight he'd just come down, pushing past the weeping tea-girl, and at the double doors which ended the flight below, two large porters were coming through. There was no sign of Shofiq, though, that was one thing : the crafty get must have scarpered all right.

Bernard turned to his left and pelted along a corridor. He didn't have much idea what he was up to, and he didn't have much hope of getting away. He just ran along, and when the people behind him came off the stairs onto his corridor, he ducked left down another one. About fifty feet along were some double doors, marked 'Social Services Department'. Ah well, he thought, it's all the same to a man on the run. He pushed them open and darted through.

He realised at once that he'd made a mistake, but by then it was too late. Instead of an escape route he'd run straight into the lion's den. It was a large, light room, full of desks and typewriters. About twenty surprised faces turned towards him as he stood there puffing.

'Hey!' said one at last. 'Hey, you! What are you doing here?'

Bernard spun round on his heel, ready to bomb off through the door and try some other way. Then another voice spoke to him.

'Good God, I *know* you! Aren't you . . . aren't you . . .'

Bernard knew who it was, even if the man couldn't remember *his* name. He shrugged and gave up. You couldn't beat fate, everyone knew that.

'What *are* you doing here, boy?' asked Mr Burke, as Bernard turned to face him. 'Why are you panting? You'd better come with me.'

# Chapter Fifteen

BERNARD looked at Mr Burke and Mr Burke looked at Bernard. All around them typists and young men in posh trousers and coloured shirts looked at both of them. Bernard glanced back at the double doors, half-expecting them to burst open and the hordes of people to come roaring in. He wished he'd really had a Luger under his arm. He'd blast this little tubby get from here to Tuesday week.

'I don't want to come with you,' he said. 'I want to get out. I didn't do nowt wrong, it was all her fault, that stuck-up crow upstairs.'

Mr Burke, who had been smiling, went a different colour. He said to another man, who'd come up beside him : 'Mind if I borrow your office for a minute, Tom ? I don't want to have to go all the way to Gateway.'

The man nodded, and Mr Burke waved Bernard towards a room. Bernard didn't move, until the double door suddenly *did* swing open. Then he changed his mind. There seemed to be millions of them out there – after him. He hopped past Mr Burke with a scared look over his shoulder.

'Wait there, boy, and don't touch anything,' said Mr Burke. 'I'll just find out exactly what's been going on.'

Once the door was closed, Bernard figured he'd made the wrong choice. But it was too late, that was that. Outside the office he could hear voices, quite a few of them, and pretty excited. He stared at the handle, willing it not to ping down and the door to open. The voices got quieter. He looked about him, to see if there was another door out. There wasn't.

The office was big, and light, with huge windows that looked over the town. When his heart had slowed down to something like normal he wandered around it. Big desk, with lots of papers on it and some photographs of a soppy-looking woman and two posh kids. A couple of pens in a holder and a file marked 'Rosetree', which was the name of one of the worst estates in the town, where the real bad lads lived. He was going to open it to have a peep, but he came to his senses just in time. Eh up, Bern, he thought, aren't you in enough ruddy lumber just for today, like?

Mr Burke seemed to be out for ages. He wandered over to the windows and stared through. The sky was washed-out, clean, with a few clouds here and there, moving fast. It would be dead good in his submarine tonight, with this wind. It had been a bad winter in the Atlantic this year; good fun. He studied the street below, one of the biggest main roads in the town, that ran all the way from Manchester in one direction to Leeds or somewhere over the tops. It was hell's busy, jammed with trucks and buses and that. People too, all wrapped up in their winter woollies and their scarves, trudging about. No sign of Shofiq though; by, he was a crafty one, that. He was a better spy even than Bernard, maybe. He must ask him how long he'd been at it.

His eyes were wandering over the rest of the town – a queer mixture of old buildings and mills with tall chimneys in the background, and sort of dirty grey new ones nearer, all glass and concrete that had been white till the local grime got to it – when the door opened. He looked back into the room. He was sweating, but not from fear, merely from heat. It was terribly hot in the office, about a million degrees. It was ridiculous.

'Well,' said Mr Burke, in a jovial fashion. 'I think I've

managed to save your neck from the noose this time. But it was a close-run thing, let me tell you, a close-run thing. What's your name, lad?'

'If you'd been listening the other night, 'appen you'd have heard, like,' Bernard said. It sounded rude, dead rude, and he meant it to. The little chubby man had a right false smile on, a real, grown-up 'You can trust me, lad' smile. Bernard wouldn't have trusted him as far as he could spit. No, not that far even, not by a long chalk: Bernard was a jolly good spitter.

Mr Burke was sweating. He ran his finger round the inside of his tight collar and wiped it on the leg of his trousers. He smiled again.

'My my, we are spiky, aren't we?' he said. 'Well, there's no need for me to know, no need at all.'

'It's Bernard Kershaw,' said Bernard. 'And you've got nothing on me, mister. I knocked over a tea tray, all right, but that weren't my fault, she were in the way that's all. I said sorry, too,' he added. 'And I picked up her specs off the floor.'

'Bernard Kershaw,' said Mr Burke. He thought for a while. 'Not a name I know. You're not one of our lot, are you? You or your family?'

Bernard looked blank. Now what was the twerp on about? Mr Burke laughed.

'No, I can see you're not,' he said. 'Well now, tell me all about it. Our Miss Merridew was most upset. She says you called her some rather terrible things. Was that entirely necessary, I wonder?'

Bernard was at a loss. Why couldn't this fellow talk English? Necessary? Necessary? He shook his head.

'I don't follow,' he said. 'Who's this Miss Merrything, anyway? I said nowt to no one that they didn't deserve.'

The chubby man sat down on a low, squodgy armchair. Black plastic again, or maybe this one was leather. It was dead plush, anyway, not like the seats in the hall. A pity that little lass hadn't peed on this one, he thought. Might of taught Slimepot a lesson. Slimepot pointed at a hard chair for Bernard to sit. He ignored him.

'Now listen here, boy,' said Mr Burke, in a less friendly tone. 'I don't entirely know what this is all about, and why you are here at all. But I'd rather like to find out. For starters we'll have less of your cheek, and you can begin by telling me why you're at these offices this afternoon instead of being at school.'

Bernard grinned. This bloke were soft, no danger, didn't know nothing.

'They wouldn't let us in, mister,' he said cheekily. 'Kept us locked out in the cold. Terrible, ain't it?'

Mr Burke was rapidly beginning to look sick. He'll lose his temper in a minute, thought Bernard. He'd never make a teacher, he'd be tore to pieces by the rougher kids.

'Now listen, boy,' said Mr Burke. Bernard smiled, a smile that said 'play a different record, do'.

'It's election day, mister,' he said. 'They're using our school, see. So we got a buckshee day. It's amazing, ain't it?'

The man drew in a couple of deep breaths.

'I'm beginning to see what Miss Merridew meant,' he said. 'You are one of the cheekiest little beggars I've met for quite some time. All right, I'm fed up trying to be friendly with you. You're in bad trouble, do you know that? Why did you say it?'

'Say what, sir?' said Bernard politely. He was in a reckless mood, a funny mood, as though he couldn't really control what he was saying. It wasn't pleasant, he was dead nervy, but he didn't seem to be able to stop it. Despite himself, almost, he put on a mock-sorrowful face, as if he was sorry for being rude. He could see it made the social work man wild, he began drumming his fingers on the desk. There was a pause.

'Listen, lad,' said Mr Burke, for about the third time. 'I understand you are a friend of young Ahmed Rahman's. Well if you are, and if you want to help him, I can assure you you are going *exactly* the wrong way about it. *Exactly* the wrong way.'

This shut Bernard up. He started to feel not so good. He bit his lip. Truth to tell, he'd almost forgotten Shofiq's problems. That's what they'd come to sort out.

'As I understand it from Miss Merridew,' went on the man, 'Ahmed Rahman came seeking information. I assume it *was* Ahmed, as he was with you. He came to entirely the wrong place, of course, and Miss Merridew, with the best will in the world, was unable to help. Children should perhaps not meddle where . . . well, never mind.' He coughed, running his finger round his sweaty collar again.

'When Miss Merridew informed Ahmed that she couldn't help, she tells me, he took it reasonably sensibly. At least he was not impolite. But as for you . . . To put it mildly, you used bad language. Vile language, dirty and disgusting language. Why?'

Bernard racked his brains to remember what he'd said. He couldn't, but he was right sure it hadn't been dirty and disgusting. Why were grown-ups such terrible liars, he wondered. Why did they say something like he'd said was dirty when they all said worse things to each other all the time?

'So you don't want to answer, eh?' said the chubby man. 'Very well, lad. But will you answer me this? *What* were you doing here, the pair of you? What did you hope to achieve? I am helping Rahman's family and I have been for some little time. As you must know, his mother is ill and his oldest sister is not helping things a scrap. We will be able to make everything better, we will look after everybody as they need it. Why should you two come along here and make a lot of trouble for all concerned?'

Bernard was amazed. This little fat creep was sitting there with a smug look on his face and telling him he was *helping*. He couldn't believe it. His weird, cheeky mood disappeared. It was flooded out.

137

'You're not helping!' he said. He tried to stop himself but it all came tumbling through. 'You're not helping at all! You're driving 'em all potty with sticking your nose in. You don't even know Shofiq's ruddy name! You can't even get his ruddy *name* right!'

'Shofiq?' said Mr Burke. 'Oh I . . . Ahmed . . .'

'Yeah, that's it, ain't it?' said Bernard. 'Ruddy Ahmed! His name's Shofiq. Shofiq! Shofiq! And he's a Pakistani, get it, a Pakistani! Not a bloody Paki like that . . . that . . . that *cow* upstairs called him.'

He was almost crying.

'How dare you!' said Mr Burke, playing the grown-up game again, shocked like mad over damn all.

'I don't know,' cried Bernard, sitting down suddenly. 'I don't know!' He was starting to bawl, tears were squirting out of his eyes and washing down his face. A big bubble of snot came out of his nose as he snorted, and he wiped it all over his face and his anorak sleeve.

'You're all the ruddy same,' he said. 'He's done nowt wrong, none of 'em have. His mum's not barmy, she's just ill, that's all, and you're hounding 'em, you're driving 'em crackers. And now his dad's got sack and you'll get even worse on 'em. I know it, Shofiq knows it, and we come along to help, that's all. To help, not to cause trouble.'

He was bawling so hard now, he had to pause, snorting and bubbling, trying to catch his breath.

'And then . . . and then . . . and then that snooty bitch called him a Paki,' he said. 'And she were right nasty to a poor old feller of ninety what couldn't talk right, and then she called my mate a rotten Paki. It's not fair! It's not *fair*!'

He subsided, rubbing his face frantically with his sleeve. He couldn't see Mr Burke's face properly, but it looked pretty grim.

'Now that just isn't true, you know,' said Mr Burke. 'Miss Merridew *certainly* did not call your friend a . . .

Paki. She would certainly have said Pakistani, make no doubt of that. That just is not true.'

Bernard would have screamed, but he was gulping too much. He almost burst with fury and hatred.

Mr Burke said: 'If you genuinely believed you heard that word, then you might be . . . well, being a bit upset, that's fair enough. But you were wrong, lad. Miss Merridew most certainly did not say that. Granted, we all sometimes get a little . . . well . . . it's hard for you to understand. This job . . . the language barriers . . . frustration . . . Well. But I can assure you. It's just not possible that a girl . . . that anyone here . . .'

He tailed off. Even through Bernard's tears he looked quite grey, old and tired. Then he shrugged, seemed to shake something off, got very businesslike again. He said briskly: 'Tell me, though. What did you just say about Ahm . . . about Rahman's father's job?'

He hurt himself quite badly, did Bernard, as he blundered blindly out of the office. He banged the top part of his leg against the drawer of a filing cabinet that had been left open. He must have been a fair old sight as he barged through the big office, with all the typing girls and the lads in their trendy suits, but he didn't care. As he'd got up off his chair Mr Burke had been starting the rigmarole about wanting to help again. Children didn't know what they were doing, didn't realise how serious and difficult it all was, and they'd get into deep water. Bernard was getting out, that's all he knew. He had to get out.

There was a shout from the office door behind him, and he saw one or two blurry white faces. But no one stopped him. He was through the double doors, along the corridors, down the stairs and in the street in one minute flat. He almost got run down crossing the main road, skriking like a little kid, but the bus managed to brake. He ran down a back alley and hid in an entry and blubbered.

When he'd got himself more or less right again, Bernard began to think. He started to wander round the centre of the town, aimlessly, trying to work out a plan of campaign. Every now and again he'd stop to look in the window of a sports shop, or a motorbike shop, or a toy shop, but he didn't take much in. He'd done terrible things, said terrible things, and he'd obviously made everything a thousand times worse.

At first, walking up and down the wide, noisy, crowded shopping streets, he'd half expected to find Shofiq lurking for him. Every time he saw a Pakistani kid he felt his stomach jump, but after the first seven or eight disappointments he realised it wasn't going to happen. Where would Shofiq have gone, that was the question. What would he have done? Maybe he'd walked back down the Brook, but surely his dad would be home to look after the kids today. If he was finishing at the Regal even tomorrow, which was a Friday, he'd not have left home this early to start work tonight. He half resented Shofiq's dad as having been the cause of the disaster, for not going to Century House himself. Then he remembered how Miss Merridew had treated the old guy who couldn't make himself understood. He realised just how Mr Rahman must feel about these things. He'd looked such a nice-seeming little feller, too. Such a quiet, wouldn't-hurt-a-fly sort of chap. Anyway, even if Shofiq had gone home he couldn't follow him there. The things he'd done! Oh my God, maybe Shofiq would never want to talk to him again!

He would have liked to have gone and asked their Wendy what to do, but it was only a dream. Her school wasn't off for the election and she'd only tell him not to worry, anyway. She wasn't a magician, even if she was dead smart. His father? He gave a snort of unfunny laughter. Whatever the ins and outs of who was sacking who, his dad would hardly have much to say about Mr Rahman being out of work, now would he?

It was at this time that the full awfulness of what he'd done struck Bernard. He stopped, in the middle of a crowded pavement, unaware of bustly folk pushing their way all round him. That was why Shofiq's dad hadn't gone! No one had known, none of the Welfare and that! Mr Burke hadn't known! Bernard had been the one who told him, Bernard! He'd told the social worker that Shofiq's dad had got the sack! Oh my God, oh my God!

He racked his brains as he stumbled on through the streets. Shofiq had said it, true. He'd said it to that Miss Merrything. But she didn't know him, she didn't know him from Adam. She didn't know their family's name, and wouldn't have known to tell old Burke about it. *Bernard* had told. He'd put the tin lid on all their problems. He'd landed the family in the mire.

He hurried along, pushing past folk willy nilly. It was getting dark, and it was getting colder. He had to get back to Century House, to see what he could see. He felt the box of matches, jogging up and down in his anorak pocket. He hurried faster and faster.

Mr Burke's car was still there, in the chained-in car park at the side of the great big concrete building, but almost at the moment Bernard reached the opposite pavement he saw him come out of a glass door and go towards it. He had his furry Russian hat perched on his head, and the big sheepskin coat on. He was round and warm-looking, like a bear. He was carrying a big black business case. Two minutes later, without seeing Bernard, who had ducked behind a pillar box, he'd driven off in the pale blue Cortina.

He was going in the right direction, and Bernard played his hunch. He pelted down the main road as fast as he could till he got to Clegg Street. Then he branched off, behind the big shops, into a derelict area of old stone terraces that were coming down. This way, by cutting out one of the hills that the town was built on, he could get down the park in double quick time.

Quick it might have been, but it was still a good long way. Bernard ran and jogged, ran and jogged, not stopping even when he got the stitch. His feet were soon soaked from the muddy demolition sites he kept crossing, and his jeans were covered in mud and grime. When he got to the edge of the park it was almost dark. There was a strong wind gushing through the trees all round the open area, and nobody to be seen on it, not even a dog.

Bernard kept in the trees and low shrubs right round the edge until he got to Gateway House. It stood quite a way back from a road that went past the park, and the back of its garden was actually marked off by the bushes that Bernard was on the other side of. It was a piece of cake pushing his way through them, and there were lots of outbuildings, half-down most of them, behind the actual house. He got into one of them, that smelled of tar and stuff like that, so that he could get a good peer at the house.

About half its lights were still on, but it was almost going home time, for sure. Every couple of minutes another window went dark, and he could hear cars starting up round the other side. After a bit, when the whole of the back was dark and deserted, he went round to have a view of the parking area. Only two cars were left, both blue. One was a Renault, the other a Ford. Mr Burke's rubbish Cortina.

Five minutes later the owner of the French car, a tall, skinny woman with a coat down past her knees, came out and got in. The engine started, the lights swept the bush he was hidden in, then it was gone. He sneaked right round Gateway House then, until he saw the one lighted window left, on the top floor. Behind that window must be Burke. Planning . . . what? Something awful for Shofiq's family.

It was cold. Real freezing brass monkeys. Bernard jiggled the matches up and down in his pocket, shivering. Cold it was, fire was hot. He and Shofiq had talked about it, and he'd worked it all out, lying in his submarine. He ought to burn the place down, no danger. And it would serve that Mr Burke right if he was inside when it happened.

Bernard wandered about for nearly half an hour like this, his hand constantly playing with the matches, peering up at Mr Burke's window, looking darkly at the pale blue Cortina. He could either put a match to the whole caboodle, or chuck a rock through into the lighted office, or smash the car headlights. He tried to turn himself into Bernard of the Black Hand. He tried to see the building blazing sky-high and him telling Shofiq everything was going to be all right. At the least, at the very very least, he could use the matches to stick in Burke's valves and let his tyres down.

When Mr Burke had come out and driven off, testing the front door a couple of times to make sure it was locked, Bernard mooched home. He watched the telly listlessly, some boring cowboy film. At bed-time he just took off his plimsoll-boots and jeans – not even his jumper. He submerged the submarine immediately, without really caring about the enemy, without even noticing the buffeting wind at the bedroom window. He didn't care that his petrol engine would use up all the oxygen, he didn't even care if he forgot to close the hatch and drowned. He didn't care about anything.

# Chapter Sixteen

SHOFIQ wasn't in school the next morning, which wasn't surprising, but then, neither were his two little sisters – and that was. Bernard had hung around on the croft until he'd made himself late, watching every possible way they could have come, but they'd never showed up. He stood at the back in prayers, searching the faces of the little'uns in case he'd made a mistake, but he couldn't spot them. It meant something awful had happened, like after the ambulance do, because although Shofiq often had to miss school, and his sister was always skipping, he was dead hot on the little girls getting an education, and made them go even if they weren't properly well.

In class he got some coolish looks from Maureen and Terry and Dougie, and in playtime they ganged up to know where he'd been the day before. They'd even gone round to the flats after dinner to pick him up, because they'd reckoned on spending the afternoon down the swimming baths with some money that Dougie had saved up. In the end Maureen's mum had dragged her off to the hairdresser's too, and she'd have missed that torture if they hadn't been hanging around wondering where Bernard was. Bernard said lamely : 'It looks dead good. Mo, smashing' – which it did, cut short and bouncy – but she just told him not to be wet. She went all red, and her blue eyes looked darker and glittery.

'Don't say things like that, Bern,' said Terry. 'She'll want to kiss you next.' But he regretted it, because

Maureen banged his earhole, and she couldn't half hit.

Bernard couldn't explain what had truly happened, but he hinted that something rotten was going on. He said how he and Shofiq had had a bit of a do with the bloke in the blue Cortina and that he reckoned there was trouble brewing.

'We're going to have to go down the Brook tonight,' he said, as the buzzer went to end playtime. 'I don't know what we'll be able to do, but I reckon we've got to help. Poor old Shofiq's not in school again, and we've got to find out why.'

At dinnertime they wanted to know more, but when they turned the corner into their warm place behind the boiler shed they got a shock. Bobby Whitehead and Big Patsy Broome were standing there, with right nasty smiles on their ugly mugs. Bernard almost turned to run, because the last thing in the world he wanted now was a fight. He had trouble enough, trouble enough and a lot more. Bobby Whitehead shrieked with laughter.

'Don't scarper off, Bern!' he shouted. 'Me and Pat won't bite you, you know. There's only two of us, can't you count? And there's four of you.'

Pat Broome added: 'Not that we couldn't batter you up rotten, anyway. We're not scaredycats. But we haven't come for that.'

'Well what have you come for?' said Bernard. 'We don't want to talk to the likes of you. One big stupid bully and one big ugly old crow.'

Pat Broome went red, which was nice. She hated being called ugly, because she was.

'I'll do you, Bernard Kershaw,' she snarled. 'You dirty little blackie-lover!'

She bunched up her fists, and Bernard bunched up his. He didn't give a damn really. If there had to be a fight, there had to be. But Whitehead grabbed Patsy's arm.

'Leave off, leave off,' he said. 'You're ruddy daft, you

are, Broomey. We've come to give 'em fair warning, right? Why waste us energy now?'

'Anyway,' said Maureen, 'this is our place, so why don't you just say your piece and bomb off? We don't like the smell of pigs.'

Dougie snorted with laughter. Bernard smiled at Maureen. She looked smashing again today. She winked at him, her eyes dancing. Well, if it comes to it, he thought, the gang weren't going to scarper this time. Whitehead and Co were going to get a right battering when the balloon went up, no danger.

Well, the balloon was going to go up, that was what Whitehead and Patsy had come to say.

'Look, let's drop the messing about. Just stand still, Patsy, and leave it be. You can give Blondie a good bashing tonight, then you won't get caned for it. This is the ruddy playground you know, not the croft. Just shut up, you lot, and listen. Me and Patsy have got some news for you. Some bad news.'

Terry was about to say something funny, but it was getting boring.

'Leave it be, Terry,' said Bernard. 'Let's hear 'em out.'

The two groups faced each other. The wind blew round the shed, with a few light drops of rain. It was freezing.

'All right,' said Bobby Whitehead. 'Don't say I don't give you fair warning, Bernard Kershaw. We're out to get you, you and your pals, and we're going to give you a battering you won't never forget. And it's going to be tonight, right, after school. Are you chicken?'

'We're not chicken,' said Bernard. 'We'll eat you for rotten breakfast, Whitehead. You're a big bully, that's all, and all bullies are cowards, everyone knows that. How many have you got to bung your bricks for you? Five thousand? There's four of us.'

Bobby Whitehead smiled nastily.

'Where's your little Paki-pal then, eh? Did he get advance warning? Has he stayed off special?'

'Don't be so ruddy wet,' replied Bernard. 'Shofiq Rahman's laid you out once, Bobby Whitehead. If he was here you wouldn't even dare to fight us with an army. He half killed you last time, and next time he sees you he'll finish off the job. So think on.'

'Come on then,' said Maureen. 'How many have you got, Whitehead? I bet it's at least two dozen. Have you give Sammy Woods and Peter Winterbottom all your next week's sweeties? They must be mad, joining in with a soft get like you!'

It would have been good, in a way, if they could have riled them into a fight there and then, but it didn't work. It wasn't long before the buzzer went, and they all went off to their classes. In the afternoon playtime the gang had a conference.

'I'm not exactly feared,' said Dougie, with a long face. 'It's more terror, like. I mean, I'm not frighted, I just wish I'd been run down by a lorry on the way to school.'

'Aye,' said Terry. 'It's a bit of a pig, ain't it? I mean, there's bound to be hundreds of 'em, and we haven't even got Shofiq.'

'Listen,' said Bernard. 'There ain't going to be no fight, and that's that. That Whitehead can have got the biggest army since the blitz, but he's not going to get a crack at us. Not tonight. We're going down the Brook.'

'But he'll have told the whole school,' said Maureen. 'If we just run off we'll be a laughing stock. I'm not a ruddy coward, Bern. I'm not feared of that ugly crow Broome, no, nor of Whitehead, neither. I vote we wade in.'

It's crazy this, thought Bernard. Till Shofiq came on the scene this gang was a ruddy joke, they wouldn't have fought an army of mice, or flies even. They've gone fight-mad. But what would they do when they actually *saw* Whitehead and Co with an armful of wallbricks each? And Sammy Woods, and Peter Winterbottom, and a couple of other great thugs? Anyway, it just weren't on. There were too many other problems.

'Listen,' he said. 'And don't argue. I'm telling you, we're going down the Brook tonight, and we're going to find out what's up with Shofiq. That's that and all about it. If you lot want to stay and have your heads battered in, fair enough. But you'll do it without me. So make up your minds. I'm going down the Brook.'

Dougie grumbled: 'I don't know what's worse. I mean down the Brook's full of Paki . . . stanis' – he just got the ending on in time – 'and that. I mean, it's dead dangerous down there at night.'

It clinched it. All the others rounded on him for that. Shofiq was *all* their mates, and for wet Dougie to say a thing like that! Ruddy hell, Bern practically lived down there these days – and nights! Had he come to any harm?

What they needed, at the end of the day, was a bit of luck in the batches Miss Todd let them out of class in. If they all got out at once they could do a quick whip round all the doors and gates to see which one was the safest, then they could be away before the Whitehead gang had a chance to corner them. What they got was the worst luck possible. She let them out, all four of them, in separate batches. Because the duty teacher never let you hang around in the cloakroom, and because the first out was Dougie, who wasn't as bright as he might have been, the whole thing was a disaster. Dougie got on his anorak and went out into the playground, where Bernard found him stood right in the middle, in full view of all the gates. Bobby Whitehead's little'uns, acting as spies, passed on their reports, in excited squeaks. By the time Terry and Maureen were out, the gang was waiting for them, their faces already flushed with victory. Whichever gate Bernard's lot ran for, they could head them off.

Bernard became a great general, in his head, immediately. He became Rommel, who although he was on the wrong side was reckoned by his dad to have been the greatest general of all, and a good bloke too. General Bernard Rommel hit on a move of complete brilliance.

148

'Follow me,' he hissed, and he started to run. To everyone's amazement, he ran not for a gate, but back into the school. Dougie was terrified, but followed. Maureen and Terry were amazed, but they followed also. It was unheard of. They'd get into terrible trouble.

They pelted into the school, along a corridor, and straight past the staff-room. Incredibly, no teacher came out. They pelted down another corridor, round a corner, and into the hall. Through the windows they could see Whitehead's mob, in confusion, all jumbled round one gate.

'Right,' said Bernard Rommel. 'Get these tanks out of here! Down the end, turn right, and out the Middleton Road gate.'

As they clattered off, there was a shout behind them. They faltered, the voice was the worst in the school. As they stared at him, Mr Ellis did his famous trick. He went from being a normal colour to red, to brick-red, to purple, to black in about nought seconds flat.

'You!' he shouted. 'Come here!'

Bernard gave Maureen a huge shove in the back that nearly knocked her clean through the door.

'Run!' he shrieked. 'Just run!'

Mr Ellis was roaring like a bull behind them, but it was too late for messing about. In seconds they were back in the playground and haring for the Middleton Road gate. The Whiteheads started streaming across the playground after them, but stopped in a dismayed bunch when the headmaster burst out of the school in front of them. By the time they'd bombed back through the gate they'd come in by and run right round the outside of the school fencing to get onto Middleton Road, Bernard and his lot had got a good start.

Bernard's decision to become General Rommel was a great one. The route they took down the Brook wasn't the quickest by any means, but it was main roads nearly all the way. Even though Whitehead, Big Patsy, Sammy

Woods and Peter Winterbottom could run faster than any of them, being bigger, they were completely unable to open fire. If they'd started chucking rocks at the four racing kids on the street with people and cars and everything about, they'd have been nabbed in seconds. They caught up steadily, with the stream of little'uns behind them growing longer and longer as they got tired and slowed down. But never a shot was fired.

The way Bernard led was very similar to the one he'd chased Shofiq along the night they'd become mates. The last stretch of it was down a long hill, and into a far less busy area. As the number of people all around them dwindled, the danger of Whitehead and Co being able to start hurling bricks at them got greater and greater. It was Maureen who realised the other terrible thing. It led to a dead, end.

'Hey, Bern,' she panted. 'What are you doing, lad! This leads to railway. We'll get cut off!'

Bernard was almost too puffed to answer.

'Give over,' he gasped. 'Give over and run.'

There was a clattering, and the first stone skittered along the pavement past their feet.

'Run!' shouted Bernard.

Round the next bend, down the slope, was the high concrete wall round the railway. They raced towards it like four steam engines, clouds of breath bursting out before them and streaming behind. The wall came closer and closer, closer and closer. But there were no more stones. Bobby Whitehead probably figured there was no rush any more. General Rommel had made his fatal mistake.

One last, light corner to the left, past the final row of boarded up terraces, and the lower, tumbledown wall of St Peter's churchyard came into view.

'There!' gasped Bernard. 'Over the wall, Terry, quick. There's a low bit just along. The stones are down.'

They skidded to a stop, panting and sweating like mad.

'In there!' squeaked Dougie. 'In St Peter's! You're puddled you are, Kershaw, you're right steaming potty puddled. You must be ruddy mad!'

'Shut up and get over,' gasped Bernard. 'Or stay if you like. I've been in there and it's a cinch. Not a ruddy ghost in sight. But if you stay out here, lad, *you'll* be a ghost, no danger!'

'Give us a bunk-up, quick,' said Terry. 'I can hear that Bobby Whitehead's lot. Give us a push.'

'They'll not come in here for sure,' said Maureen, giving Terry a shove up the loose rocks. 'They'll wonder where we've gone to!' Terry pulled her up and they both helped Bernard.

Dougie dithered for five seconds longer. The other three looked down at him.

'You're a right dumpling, you,' said Maureen scornfully. 'What a ruddy brother!'

'Ah, to hell with it,' said Dougie. He took a running jump at the wall and they hauled him up and over.

'Good lad,' said Maureen. 'You're a right smasher really, our Doug!'

Bernard led the way, and he never slowed down. It wasn't quite as dark as last time he'd been in, but he warned them to go carefully in case of falling down and hurting themselves on the loose and broken tombstones. For all that, though, they shot through the place like a dose of salts. He may not have seen a ghost last time, but it must've been more by luck than judgement. The trees sighed, the broken crosses and mouldy old angels seemed to move in towards them, and the great pile of the derelict church was worse than a hundred horror films.

When they got to the other side, when they were truly down the Brook, they paused and listened. Faintly, behind them, they could hear shouting. They hung about for a few seconds or so, but it didn't get louder. They'd done them, absolutely no danger. Whitehead and Co probably wouldn't dare come into Little India, most kids wouldn't. And to come across the churchyard as well! Impossible.

They ran towards Cardigan Road, following Bernard, chattering excitedly among themselves. They felt great, fantastic. They'd done Whitehead proper, and they'd showed the ghosts a thing or two into the bargain. The Kershaw mob were a great mob, no doubt of that. They were utterly fan-ruddy-tastic!

When they got to the last alleyway, that would lead them out almost opposite Shofiq's house, they slowed down. They weren't panting any more, and they could hear a noise in front of them. It was a peculiar noise, lots of voices, but nothing you could put a name to. They looked at each other, puzzled, but no one spoke. Then they crept down the alley almost fearfully, wondering what the heck they could be going to see.

What they saw was a mystery. The street was full of people, jammed with them. They were Pakistanis, almost all of them. Men in cheap suedette jackets, lots of women in long white dresses, or silk pyjama things. There was one little kid out, wearing only a tee shirt and a pair of slippers, in all that freezing cold, looking lost.

The crowd was centred on a couple of cars outside Shofiq's house. They were milling round them. One Bernard recognised immediately, the moment he saw it through a gap. It was Mr Slimepot Burke's blue Cortina.

Everyone recognised the other one. It was white, and fluorescent red, with a blue flashing light on top, going round, and round, and round.

'Oh cripes,' said Bernard. 'Oh blistering cripes. It's the police.'

# Chapter Seventeen

THEY stood there for what felt like an age, completely at a loss as to what to do. They kept in the shadows watching. The scene was weird, horrible. Practically everyone in the street must have been out, grouped round the two cars. There was noise, the confused noise the kids had heard from the alley, but it wasn't loud any more, and it was getting softer. The people were talking to each other, in low voices. They didn't even appear to want to get too close to the police; they just stood about, looking somehow crushed, and hopeless. It was amazing how much alike all the men looked, all in dead cheap dark suits and shoes off the market, plastic or cheap cardboardy leather, some of them wearing these short over-jackets, like Mr Burke's only imitation, mostly a ginger pretend-suede stuff. The women were somehow quite different, some in robes, some with covered faces, some in silk trousers.

A lot of the noise was coming from by Shofiq's front door, by the house, so Bernard started forward, with the others keeping close behind him. As they pushed into the crowd, which melted to either side as the white kids came through, they could hear shouting, very confused shouting. The blue lamp on the cop car kept going round, lighting up the fronts of the terraces, and the faces, making them go a funny colour as it passed over. They heard loud English voices, which must have been the police. They heard a high, sort of broken voice, talking a sort of English that was more like Chinese, only with a Pakistani accent: Shofiq's dad, for sure. And then they heard Shofiq.

He was practically screaming.

'No!' he said. 'No you can't! It's not allowed! You musn't do this!'

Then there was some more English talk, a lower rumble.

The faces of the people in the crowd did not show surprise as Bernard and Maureen and Terry and Dougie pushed through. They didn't show any emotion at what was going on. It was most peculiar, Bernard thought: they were like sad, silent statues.

When they got to the front, Bernard tried to take in exactly what was happening. The police car was pulled up behind Mr Burke's Cortina, both of them outside the Rahman's front door. One of the panels in the door was smashed, and there was light spilling out of it into the street. In the light he could see Mr Burke's face, and it was a queer sight. There was a smear of blood all down one cheek, and what looked like a cut in the flesh over his right eye. He still had his daft Russian hat on, but it was pushed sideways over his ear, as if someone had belted him. His face was white and angry, turning blue every few seconds when the cop car flasher swept over it. There was blood on the nice white furry collar of his expensive sheepskin.

All this pleased Bernard somewhat, then he picked out Mr Rahman behind two policemen. They were holding him by his arms, and alongside them he looked tiny, like a little doll. He had on a pair of black trousers and a sort of dirty-yellow cardigan thing, and his hair, lank and shiny with grease, had fallen down over his forehead. He was talking, not loudly, and struggling in the grip of the monster coppers. As the blue light passed over he lifted his head, and Bernard saw it was soaking wet. He was also making a horrible gulping noise in between words. Shofiq's father was crying!

Shofiq himself was leaning against the wall beside the front door at this moment, sobbing into the brickwork. He was still in his black jeans and green jumper, and it looked as though he'd given up hope for the minute. Bernard heard one of the coppers say to Mr Rahman: 'I do wish you'd belt up for a while, mate. You'll have to come with us now, and that's that.'

There was another policeman in the car, and he turned to glance over his shoulder. Bernard followed the movement. In the back of the car sat Shofiq's queer sister, staring straight in front like a zombie. The two tiny girls were wrapped round each other, howling fit to bust.

Shofiq suddenly pushed himself off the brick wall and launched himself at Mr Burke's fat stomach. He bounced off it, then back again, trying to pummel it with his fists. He was shrieking.

'No! No! No! You've got to leave us alone! You've got to leave us alone! You can't take my father away!'

Mr Burke grabbed him by the wrists, shaking him hard. He had a grim smile on his white face, his 'Come come, I know what's best' smile.

'Now now, Ahmed,' he said. 'Do be a good boy. It's all for the best, you know. It's the only way.'

'It's not the only way,' shrieked Shofiq. 'It's *your* way, that's all. It's nothing to do with us, it's to ruddywell suit you! It's *your* ruddy way!'

His father yelled something then, something that Bernard couldn't catch; couldn't even tell what language it was in, English or foreign.

One of the policemen said loudly: 'Now come along! Enough's enough. There's been an assault here and you've to come with us. That's it and all about it.'

Mr Rahman started to struggle. He wriggled and shook like a cat that's been grabbed by a toddler. The two big cops pushed and hustled him towards the car. The man in the front leaned behind him and shoved open the back door. Mr Rahman started yelling right loud, really roaring, as they pushed him in. One of the coppers lost his cap. You could see by their faces they'd be losing their tempers before long. In a few seconds they managed to shove him in, one of them piling in the back as well.

The social worker still had Shofiq by the wrists. He was standing there, tears streaming down his face, all limp. The policeman walked over to them.

'I'd better take him in the front with me,' he said. 'Not a good idea for you to try and keep him in your car, eh?'

Mr Burke shook his head.

'Not a good idea at all,' he said. 'The little devil.'

On an impulse Bernard shouted.

'Hi!' he said. 'Hi, Shofiq! Over here! Run lad! Run for your life!'

Shofiq, the social worker, and the policeman all looked round at the same instant. But Shofiq's wits were the quickest by a long chalk. He jerked back his arms, flung his body to one side, and was away. As the five kids pelted through, the crowd opened like magic. There was a bellow of rage from the copper, and a higher yell of fury from Mr Burke. In a matter of seconds they'd cleared the edge of the watching street folk and they had their heads down for the all-time record-breaking Olympic sprinting championship.

Shofiq knew the streets round there best, so Shofiq led the way. Whether it was accidental or not, the crowds of people seemed to close up after they'd gone through, so by the time the copper and Mr Burke had got clear the kids had a fair lead. At first Shofiq took them straight up Cardigan Road, across a junction, then along another straight stretch. Bernard was getting worried, because grown-ups could probably catch up with them on the straight, but about then Shofiq did a sudden jink to the left and up a dark little back road with hardly any lights in it. Just as they reached the next turning, to the right, the policeman appeared at the corner behind them.

He shouted: 'Come back, you daft little gets. You'll only get yourselves in lumber!'

As they belted round to the right, Bernard saw Mr Burke come flying round too. He'd lost his furry hat and he was blowing like a clapped-out car. It wouldn't be long before they lost that one, no danger!

The copper was a different matter though. He might've sat on his bottom all day in a big fast prowl car, but he was fit, for all that. They twisted and turned in and out of crummy little streets, some of them even with cobbles down instead of tarmac. But his boots kept right behind them, and they sounded louder all the time. Every now and then he gave a shout, although they were too puffed to even speak themselves. He must've been the ruddy police champion!

Bernard reckoned they'd soon be on their last legs, when Shofiq bombed round into a really small and dark little road. They thundered along it, till they could see a rickety old wooden fence right across the end. It was high, but not that high they couldn't get over it.

'Canal,' gasped Shofiq. 'Get over quick. Canal!'

They scrambled over in twos, picking up a couple of good scratches each, and Maureen tearing a lump out of her yellow anorak sleeve. On the other side it was muddy, with tons of old junk lying around everywhere. They charged along the path beside where the water had been once, till Shofiq hissed: 'Down here. Follow me down. It's all right.'

Behind them they could hear the copper thundering at the wooden fence. The way Shofiq was pointing, down into the stinking slimy bottom of the empty canal, looked awful. But there was no need to tell them twice. They slipped and slithered after him, up to their ankles, almost, in the filth. He led them into a sort of dug out recess in what had once been the side of the canal. It stank something awful.

'Rats,' gasped Dougie. 'There'll be rats!'

'Shut up,' said Bernard, through clenched teeth. 'Shut up and keep quiet. Get your breaths. Everyone. Breathe quiet.'

The old canal side hung above them, slimy and dripping. The water and mud underfoot was evil-smelling and icy-cold. Every now and again there were small splashes, things running. Rats for certain; for a thousand pound.

After a short while they heard the policeman's cautious footsteps, saw the gleam of his torch. He flashed it all over the other bank. It showed up water, and mud, and old bikes and prams, even a soaking, filthy mattress someone had chucked out. His boots must have passed within two feet of their heads. The steps faded away, slowly, very slowly.

Shofiq whispered, in a tiny, tiny whisper: 'There's a ruined mill, the Newport. He'll think we're in there. It's a good place to hide.'

They waited a while longer. Then Shofiq whispered again.

'Give us a second,' he said. 'I'll go and have a peek.'

He scrambled up the canal bank and stared about.

'He's in the mill,' he said. 'I can see his torch. Come up quick, and let's scarper. But quiet, dead quiet. Give us your mitt, Maureen, I'll hoick you up.'

They crept back across the towpath and along a stretch of rotting wall, trembling with terror in case the copper came out before they could find the gap Shofiq was searching for. Then they got it. They squeezed through, one by one, and were back on a side-street of boarded up houses.

'Let's get,' said Bernard. 'I vote we try the main road for a bit. Get out of the Brook sharpish.'

'Rubbish,' said Maureen. 'You're talking daft, Bern. The police'll be all over the big roads leading out, they've got radios. We'd never get past. We'll have to go the park way. Even if they see us then, we can scatter. They'll never catch us if we scatter. It stands to reason.'

It was true, no argument. But to get to the park they had to go on the main road at least some of the way. They walked fast, like a forced march, until they reached the big road, then prepared to run like hell for the rest of the way.

They'd just poked their noses out to make sure the way was clear when they heard a sound that nearly made them die of fright. The two-tone blaring of a police car siren. They pressed themselves flat into the doorway of the closed-down corner shop, and the car went by. Its headlights were full on, and inside it they could see four policemen glaring about.

After it had gone they looked at each other in fear. But there was nothing for it, no other way. They got onto the road and ran as fast as they could towards one of the entrances to the park. The hunt was up – with a vengeance.

When they reached the track that led straight down to the dark open space, however, they knew they'd missed their chance. Not one but two police cars were parked down there. And they could make out dark figures walking across the grass, occasionally flashing torches on and off into bushes. They turned to go back, to try by the main roads, dangerous or not. But even as they turned they saw another car nosing down. Its lights were full on, blinding, and it was going very slow. It *must* be the police again.

There was only one other way out, and they all knew it. They started to make for the churchyard, quickly and quietly, keeping their eyes peeled for the men in blue. It was full dark now, a real, black, freezing, overcast night. They weren't afraid of the coppers so much as the ghosts now, now it was so pitchy black, but there was no other way out. Even Shofiq, who they'd reckoned didn't worry about English ghosts, was tense and miserable-seeming. He hardly opened his mouth to say a word any more.

They picked their way carefully through the smashed-up old graves, pressed as close together as they could get. Some of the biggest slabs had slipped sideways, or been smashed up by the bad lads and vandals, so that the holes right deep into the ground where the coffins must lie were all open. It would be the easiest thing in the world for a vampire to get out if he'd a mind to; the front door was left ajar, so to speak.

What they hadn't bargained for, what had never even entered their heads as a danger, was what actually happened.

Shofiq had got more and more miserable as time went on, he seemed to be chewing over in his head all the awful things that had happened with the police and the social worker outside his house, and the others had got more thoughtful as he did. They were in a terrible mess, one way and another, and everything they did seemed to make it worse. Here they were, wandering through a haunted graveyard at night, and if they weren't done in by the spooks, what then? You'd hardly say the prospects looked bright: at home, talking to their mums and dads would be bad, and even more terrible to think on was school on Monday. It was frightening.

But everything changed when they jumped one by one over the low part of the wall onto the road by the railway. For although it had felt like ages to them, while all of the excitement and misery had been going on, it couldn't have been so long at all. Bobby Whitehead, Big Patsy Broome, Peter Winterbottom, Sammy Woods, were all still there. So was Georgie Greenwood, so was Freddie Wright, and so was Bertie Smith, along with half a dozen more of the littler kids that hung around with Whitehead and Co. And each and every one of them had a pile of wallbricks at his feet, and each and every one of them was ready with one to chuck.

It was a complete and utter disaster.

As they stood in front of the graveyard wall, blinking in the dim light of the street lamps, that was still a hundred times brighter than the churchyard, Bobby Whitehead gave an absolute yell of triumph that his gamble had paid off and told his troops to open fire. They'd been waiting a long time on the off chance, and they'd collected a mixture of stones, glass chunks, bits of brick and the odd lump of metal, in case Bernard and his lot did ever come back. They let fly as one man, and the hail of missiles was fantastic.

Often in brickfights, Bernard had noticed, the sides stood so far apart that there wasn't actually that much chance of anyone getting badly hit. But this time, because of the length of time Whitehead had had to plan, and because of the high concrete railway wall behind his gang, the range was very short. In the first volley Bernard was hit three times, once in the leg, once in the stomach, and once on the shoulder. The shoulder one was worst, it must have been half a wallbrick, and the pain was terrible. He half turned, back towards the graveyard, and shouted: 'Run! Get back in St Peter's! Run!'

Another rock hit him then, above the right ear, and he felt blood dribbling down into his anorak neck. The noise was terrible, Dougie was screeching blue murder beside him, and the row from Whitehead's lot was fantastic. They were yelling with delight, picking and throwing without a pause, starting to move slowly forward. He saw Dougie scrabbling up the ruined wall, then falling down, bringing bits of stone and rock with him. For a split second he saw Dougie's face. He was crying, and there was blood coming from a cut on his cheek.

Bernard turned round again, trying to make himself a leader, trying to turn it back into a fight. Opposite him it looked like a horde though, there were hundreds of them, and you could see the bricks and that in the sky, flying, like a solid mass of stuff flashing in the light. Something sharp hit him above the knee. He heard Dougie scream again.

He looked at Shofiq, and at last it had happened. In

the street light, whether it was real or not, his face had gone white; as pale as death. Bernard had a red surge of rage inside him. They couldn't do this to his mate: they couldn't.

He bent quickly and picked up a lump of rock the size of a baby's head. He pulled back his arm and hurled it, so hard that his elbow hurt.

'Fight!' he yelled. 'Fight! Fight!'

Terry was looking lost and frightened, Dougie was crouching by the wall, Maureen and Shofiq were shaking their heads from the pain of repeated blows. Bernard picked up a rock and shoved it at Shofiq.

'Fight!' he shouted. 'Chuck it, Shofiq, chuck it! Don't let 'em get you, lad, any of 'em! Chuck it!'

Shofiq did. Without his face changing he buzzed the rock flat and hard. There was a scream, a definite scream, from Whitehead's side. Terry suddenly grinned and mouthed some words that Bernard didn't catch, although he knew damn well what they were. Then Terry was bunging too, with great sweeps of his strong arms and a fierce smile on his face.

Whether it was to do with what his father had said, or whether it was blind rage, or panic, or madness, Bernard didn't know. But with himself and Shofiq out in front, the others close behind, they began to move forward. Bend and chuck, bend and chuck, bend and chuck. There was no point in trying to dodge, because the light wasn't good enough to properly see what was coming. He got hit lots of times, but he no longer felt the pain. Bend and chuck, bend and chuck, with Shofiq at his side. Faster and faster they moved forward, and now they were yelling louder than the enemy. Under a street light, too, he saw some of Whitehead's little'uns break away. One of them had a bloody head. He saw him drop his bricks and run.

Bernard let out a mighty whoop and hurled another lump of stone. In front of him he heard a scream, and behind him an even worse one, a really awful one. Neither of them mattered. Bobby Whitehead's gang was scattering. Peter Winterbottom suddenly scarpered, running fast up the hill and round the corner. Bobby, Big Patsy Broome and Sammy Woods stood in a straight line under a lamp post. They were hesitating, looking uncertain, frightened. Bernard gave a yell as the last of the little'uns fled. He bunged a small corner of wallbrick and saw it bounce off Patsy's forehead. He screeched with delight and she turned and fled. She chucked down her few remaining rocks and fled.

Five seconds later Whitehead and Woods followed her. Bernard looked over his shoulder and yelled to the gang to come on as he and Shofiq began to race after them. Terry and Dougie were kneeling down though, kneeling down over Maureen, who was lying curled up in the road. As he and Shofiq pelted off, bunging as many bricks as they could at Bobby Whitehead and Sammy Woods, he heard the two-tone blare of a police car, then another. They actually saw one of them go bumping off the road and onto a croft to cut off Bobby and Sam. Shofiq and Bernard, sweating, almost crying with joy and excitement, ducked down a back alley. They cut along it onto the next road, then bombed off into the dark as fast as they could.

It began to snow; or sleet really. A cold, freezing, solidifying rain.

# Chapter Eighteen

It was a long time before Bernard and Shofiq found a properly safe place to hide in, and it was there that Wendy finally ran them to earth. By that time they were hungry, miserable to the point of despair, and completely silent. There was nothing left for them to say.

After they'd routed Whitehead's gang they ran and ran, not particularly knowing where they were going. They were fantastically excited, panting and laughing and whooping as they belted along. When they passed knots of grown-ups on the lighted streets they slowed down and tried not to look too chuffed, but it was difficult. It had been a superb victory. Whitehead would never be the same again, nor any of the other bullies. Both of them had cut heads and bruised bodies, but they didn't mind.

At first they had nowhere to go, but they didn't care. They just ran aimlessly, ducking into side roads if they saw any police or police cars. They didn't feel hunted though, they felt they'd got clean away. Even the sleet, that was rapidly turning into snow as it got later, didn't worry them.

Their mood started to change when Bernard, for no real reason, turned into Bernard the Black Hand. Patting his Luger, he hit on the idea of burning down Gateway House. They were galloping along not far from that side of the park, about a quarter of an hour after the fight, when he remembered the matches.

'Hey, pal,' he shouted. 'I tell you what. Let's go and set fire to old Burke's offices. I nearly did it yesterday, after the do at the Social Security place, I did honest. I've got matches, look!'

He dragged the box out of his anorak pocket and rattled it under Shofiq's nose.

But it was wrong somehow, completely wrong. It spoiled everything. As soon as it had popped out Bernard regretted it. Shofiq slowed his pace down, went from a run to a jog, and the excited look began to fade from his face.

'Oh come on,' said Bernard, with a sinking feeling starting up inside him. 'We could do it easy. There's a shed with some tar in.'

Shofiq slowed down more and more. He stopped and stood there in the sleet. He looked a right mess, his face was bloody and cut, his jumper and jeans soaked.

'Forget it, pal,' said Bernard. 'I were only joking. It were only a joke. Come on – run.'

Shofiq looked at him. One of his cheekbones had a black bruise on it. He looked terrible.

'Where?' he said. 'Bernard. Where the hell are we going, lad?'

'Steaming heck!' shouted Bernard. He was trying to sound jolly, to sound bright. But the large empty feeling in his stomach was growing and growing. 'Hell, lad. I mean.'

They stood dripping for a while. Shofiq bit his lip.

'I reckon we'd better get down cop shop,' he said.

'What?' shrieked Bernard. 'Give ourselves up, like? You're barmy!'

'No,' said Shofiq. 'No, not that. I want to look out for me dad. See what's happened. And me sisters. Oh hell, Bernard.'

He turned about, and started to walk for the town centre. It was a long way, and he was going very slowly. Bernard walked with him. He couldn't think of anything else to do. After a while he said: 'Did he belt him? Your dad? Did he belt that Slimy Burke?'

'Yeah,' said Shofiq. 'He wanted to take . . .'

They walked a few more steps.

'What?' asked Bernard. 'What did he want to do?'

Shofiq didn't answer. His head was down. They were getting soaked to the skin.

'You'd better tell me, lad,' said Bernard. 'I'm your mate, Shofiq. I'm your best pal.' There was a funny feeling inside him, deep in his stomach. 'Better than Mickie,' he said. 'You're better than Mickie.'

After some time Shofiq said: 'They wanted to take us in care. Take us kids away from me dad, like. That Burke says he's not fit to look after us.'

Bernard said nothing. There was nothing to say, that he could think of.

Shofiq went on: 'He'd found out that me dad had lost his job. So along he came, talking about an order or something. He got on and on at me dad. He wanted to take us then, I think. Me dad got scared, frighted. He hit him.'

It was a horrible feeling, knowing that he'd done it. Shame and misery filled Bernard. He'd let it out to that Burke. It was his fault. He couldn't speak.

'It doesn't matter,' said Shofiq, just as if Bernard had blurted out the truth. 'He'd have found out soon enough any road. It doesn't matter.'

A lorry went past them, chucking filthy cold water over them from a puddle. That didn't matter either. Neither of them flinched.

'I suppose he must have been expecting a row, like,' said Shofiq. 'That cop car didn't come out of thin air, no danger. So now me dad's gone and proved it. He belted Burke and proved he weren't fit to look after his own kids. I suppose the bastards'll put him in prison now.'

'The crafty get,' said Bernard. 'The crafty horrible little get.'

'Yeah,' said Shofiq. 'It's funny, ain't it? Me dad loses

his job and that makes him unfit. Before, when he were working, Mr Burke tried to reckon he were unfit because he wasn't there to look after us. You know, like that night you come round. That's what he were up to, did you know that?'

'I don't know,' said Bernard. 'I suppose I did, when you think about it. I just don't know exactly. *Why?* Why are they trying to do it? What have they got against you?'

'I don't know,' replied Shofiq. He gave a short laugh. 'Right pair of duck-eggs we are, Bern Kershaw. We don't know nothing. Nothing at all.'

A little while later he added: 'My mum's got something to do with it. I don't know, that Burke seems to reckon that because she's ill like that, you know, in that way, in the mental home and that, that it means . . . that it shows . . . Oh hell, Bern, I don't know. It ain't fair, that's all. It just ain't fair.'

Bernard began to tremble. He walked along beside his friend without talking, but he began to tremble. Inside him something was growing that he couldn't stop. He began to shake, to feel right odd.

'Shofiq,' he said. 'My mum's like that. Like your mum, I mean, sick like that. She were going to have a kid, like. Well, she did I reckon, no one's never told me exactly what happened, like. I reckon she did have the kid and it were born dead. You know.'

Shofiq sighed.

'Aye, I know,' he said. 'It's a bad do, that.'

'Yeah,' said Bernard. They walked on. Then he added: 'She's getting worse, Shofiq. I know she is. Our Wendy and our dad say she's getting better, but she's getting worse. What I mean is . . . . well, I used to think your mum were . . . potty like. Well, all the kids said. But I reckon my mum'll have to go in St James's soon. No one's . . . no one's *never* said she's potty though. No one. I were just wondering . . . I were just wondering – why. That's all.'

The trembling inside him had died down. He was glad he'd said all this. He was glad he'd come out with it. He'd never admitted it to himself, even, before. Now he'd told his mate.

Shofiq said quietly: 'It don't matter what people say though, Bern. She *will* get better, I expect. So will my mum. It's a long job. But doctors don't tell no lies. They're not like most folk. I suppose they can be wrong, but they don't try to smash you up. Maybe they'll be in the same ward, your mum and mine. That'd be nice.'

The police station in the centre of town was a new building, quite low, with lots of glass and lights. They crept into the car park, not entirely sure of what they were doing there, hoping to see in the windows. But the windows on the ground floor were all frosted. They could see shadows moving about, but they couldn't see much else. They wandered all round the building, ducking behind cars or into doorways when any policemen were about, but it was useless. What could they do? If they went in the front they'd be arrested, just like that. But how could they find out what had happened to Mr Rahman? And the kids? What could that Slimepot Burke have done with Shofiq's sisters?

There was a lot of coming and going around the police station, cars going in and out, so they had to play it dead careful. After they'd waited for about twenty minutes they knew they'd have to move on. The sleet was properly snow now, not heavy but not messing about either. Both of them were shivering violently from time to time. Bernard's anorak had become waterlogged, so he was wet underneath it, while Shofiq's jeans and jersey were like sponges. Despite his protests, Shofiq said he'd have to go back down the Brook. The front door had got smashed in by the police, and if the house was empty, it would be robbed. Bernard tried to argue him out of it, but got nowhere. Shofiq tried to argue Bernard out of coming too, but **he** got nowhere either. This time they were going to stick together.

Before they'd got to within half a mile of his house, though, they knew they had to give up. In practically every street they tried to get down, there was a policeman or a police car. There appeared to be cars prowling everywhere, and they thanked their lucky stars the fluorescent red strips showed them up so well. The Panda cars were more of a problem, but they always spotted them in time. Fortunately most of the people that lived down the Brook didn't have cars themselves, which made the others more conspicuous. It scared them half to death though: they'd never imagined so many police would be out just to look for them.

'Cripes, Shofiq,' said Bernard. 'Anyone'd think we'd robbed a bank or something. Can all that lot really be after us?'

'I don't know,' replied Shofiq. 'But we're for it if they find us, whether or not. Come on, lad, let's scarper.'

By the time they'd got to the buildings near Bernard's flats they'd worked out that if all the activity *was* to find them, the police might have a watch on his place as well. They stood by the break in the fence and talked about it in low tones. More sense to go and hide in a half-finished house, perhaps. But they were cold, hideously cold, and if they could once get to the secret hide-out by the heating duct in the flats they could get warm again. What's more Bernard might be able to sneak indoors and get some food.

The sight of the deep, snow-covered mud across the building site decided them. They trudged on up the hill towards the flats, keeping their eyes peeled. But they saw nothing unusual, not a policeman anywhere. Presumably the police would just have told Bernard's dad to get in touch if they showed up there. It was a dead cinch. Inside the lobby Bernard had a great urge to go up and get indoors. Hot food, dry clothes, a towel. But it was out of the question. They started the long climb up the stairs in silence. They were both miserable, as miserable as sin. Even the fact that the hide-out was empty of courting couples, and much warmer than the world outside, didn't make them much happier. They sat down side by side, with their backs to the aluminium duct, trying to think what to do next. The wind howling round the high concrete building, shaking it slightly as it came blasting off the moors, sounded utterly desolate. They leaned closer together, with Shofiq's arm round Bernard's shoulder. He thought for a moment of his bed, a couple of floors away; his warm, safe, submarine. The wind howled, and he shivered violently. This was what the Atlantic must be *really* like though. Not like his submarine at all. They said not a word.

It was a great surprise to Bernard when Wendy squeezed through the narrow gap and found them. She was dressed in a long coat and her bunny-rabbit woolly hat, looking a bit on the coldish side. He'd thought this was the one place where no one knew he went, but then again it was hard to fool their Wendy. She gave them a smile, but not exactly the warmest one he'd ever had, and she spoke.

'So. Here you are at last. I've been checking. And you, Shofiq. Well well, the wanderers return.' She shook her head. 'Still in your Arctic gear eh, Shofiq? You're ruddy puddled you are, lad. Come on, out of this and I'll give you a warm.'

Neither of them tried to protest. Wendy led them to the flat and put the kettle on straight away. She chucked two towels at them and told them to get into Bernard's room and change. She said she didn't care what they put on, both of them, but she wanted them in completely dry gear, skin out, head to toe. Both of them.

'Where's me mum?' said Bernard listlessly. 'Where's me dad?'

'Your mum's in bed asleep,' said Wendy. 'Thanks to

you, our Bernard, I've had to give her another pill. You've had everybody going hairless. Your dad's down at the police station. So chew that over while you change your ruddy clothes.'

They took off their clothes in silence and dried themselves. Bernard pulled things out of a drawer and they both got into pants, vests, socks, jeans and jerseys. They were blue with cold, even when Wendy sat them down in the living room with big cups of tea and jam sandwiches. Still they said nothing. Shofiq looked like death.

Wendy had taken off her coat and hat, and she sat there staring at them. She said at last: 'I wish you hadn't of done it, our Bern. I wish you hadn't.'

He said glumly: 'We didn't do nothing. We didn't do none of it. We just went down the Brook to see what were up. To see what they were doing to Shofiq's lot. None of it weren't us.'

Bernard could tell she'd been in a terrible mood with them when she'd found them, although she hadn't shouted. But now her anger was gone. She was sad; quiet and sad.

'What's to do, our Wendy?' he asked. 'Are we to go to jail, d'you reckon? Why's our dad down cop shop? And how's Mr Rahman and the kids?'

She looked like she'd shout at him, then took a sip of her tea instead. She rubbed her forehead with her hand.

'It's a bad mess, our Bernard,' she said. 'Little Maureen McIlroy's to lose her eye.'

Bernard and Shofiq gaped. Bernard's mouth hung open; he didn't realise it for ages. They gaped.

Wendy said flatly: 'She got hit with a lump of glass they reckon. The bottom of a bottle or something. Something jagged. It's a bad mess.'

As they looked at her, she started to cry. She didn't make a noise, just let the tears roll out of her eyes, down her cheeks in floods, and off her chin onto her jumper. After a while she rubbed her eyes with her hand. She put down her cup and dried her face with a paper hankie. Bernard and Shofiq didn't move, they couldn't. Hot tea suddenly spilled all over Bernard's leg. He put his cup down.

'Your dad's all right, Shofiq,' Wendy said. Her voice was funny, as if she had something stuck in her throat. She picked up her cup and swallowed tea. 'He's down the station, but he's not being kept in I don't think. The council have took your little sisters into a home for a bit. They'll be all right, don't fret.'

Shofiq made a horrible choking sound.

'Is it definite?' he said. You could hardly hear him. 'Is it definite about Maureen? About her eye?'

Wendy shook her head. You couldn't exactly tell if she meant yes or no, but Shofiq didn't ask again.

Bernard said: 'But what about Bobby Whitehead? He started it.' He gulped. Maureen. Not Maureen. He shouted: 'He ought to go to jail! He ought to get hanged or something!' Oh my God, oh my God, he thought. He remembered Maureen's bright blue eyes, her bouncy hair.

'Shut your mouth, Bernard,' said Wendy. 'Just shut your mouth. It takes two to make a fight, even if that little sod *was* the cause of it. I expect he'll get what's due to him, when it comes down to it. And I expect you will, too.'

'I don't understand,' said Shofiq. 'It's just not fair. I just don't understand.'

He started to cry, snorting and gasping, not trying to hide it. When he'd finished, Wendy said: 'I can't help you really, lad, and that's the truth. Because I don't understand neither.' She paused for a long time, looking down into her teacup, turning it round and round in her hand.

Then she said: 'You seem a bright sort of a kid, and our Bern's all right, even if he is a bit of a cheeky twerp. What your dad's meant to have done I don't know, and why Bobby Whitehead and folk like him have got it in for you I don't know neither.'

She paused again. She kept twirling her cup slowly, her head bent. There was no tea left in it, you could tell.

'The world's full of Enochs,' she went on. 'I mean, even our dad . . . in a way, sort of . . . I mean, they just don't seem to realise. They don't know what they're up to. It's just . . . sort of ignorant. Pig-ignorant. If they *knew*. Stupid, just stupid.'

'I didn't want no trouble,' said Shofiq, brokenly. 'I didn't want no violence. My dad hit that Burke man that were hounding us, and he wouldn't hurt a fly. It's awful the things they've done to him, they wouldn't leave him alone. The whole family. Smashed up. They've smashed up the whole family. And he wouldn't hurt a fly.'

Wendy nodded slowly.

'I believe you, Shofiq, I believe you,' she said. 'It's your dad hitting the social work man that gets to be called the violence. But I wonder if they ever think what they've done to him? What's it called that's happened to your dad? Your family? And they're doing it for the best, that's the trouble, they truly believe that. They're not bad or evil men, Shofiq, you've got to understand. I expect that poor Mr Burke was breaking his neck to help really. And how else could he do it? There's laws, bound to be. There's always laws. I sometimes wonder who they're kidding most.'

'I hate him,' said Shofiq flatly. 'Whatever he did it for, whoever he thinks he's kidding, I hate him. He swamped us in the end. He proper swamped us. *That's* the violence.'

Wendy put her cup down. She stood up.

'Well, violence never works is what they say, kid. That's what we're taught in school. It hasn't worked for your dad, that's for sure. Maybe it's who does it that counts, eh? How it's organised.'

'We were organised,' said Bernard, half proudly. 'We battered the Whitehead gang to little pieces.'

Wendy went an awful colour. Her freckles stood out a glaring orange. Bernard flinched. He remembered Maureen, and felt sick.

He whispered: 'Don't hit me, our Wend. I didn't mean it, honest.'

Her eyes were hard: 'You'll get such a leathering from our dad,' she said, 'that you won't walk right for a month. And I hope it bloodywell hurts you.'

A few minutes later, when she'd got coats on both of them, and her own outdoor gear fixed up, she said to Shofiq: 'You'll go in care I expect, Shofiq. You know that, don't you? The council'll take you.'

She opened the front door, closed it behind them, and checked that it was locked. Shofiq didn't answer.

'I'm not cracking on it's going to be easy,' she said. 'But it's not the end of the world, you know. You'll get well looked after, you and your sisters, and you'll go to school and that. It's not like Borstal, or nothing. Grown-ups aren't all stupid. They're not always up the creek. They get some things right. You'll still see your dad, and your mum when she's better. And our Bernard.'

'It's me dad I'm feared for,' Shofiq said. His voice was odd; there was no tone to it, no expression. 'Maybe that Burke does believe what he's doing's right. Maybe he does think it's for our own good. But what will me dad do without me? What *can* he do? I've got to look after him, to help him. I'm the one that keeps that family going. What's going to happen to me dad?'

Bernard couldn't follow too well, but it seemed right. Wendy and Shofiq were staring at each other. They seemed to understand each other right well.

Wendy said: 'I'll tell them that, Shofiq. I'll do my best. I'll tell them that.' She rattled the front door one last time.

Shofiq said sadly: 'And d'you think they'll listen, Wendy? Do you?'

She made a funny little face, and took hold of

Bernard's hand. With her other hand, the right one, she took hold of Shofiq's.

'Come on,' she said. 'Let's go and face the music.'

Shofiq looked at her, his big eyes bright and grave.

'Are you holding me to stop me running away?' he said quietly.

'Don't be so daft,' said Wendy. 'You're Bernard's mate. I'm holding you because I like you. All right?'

A small smile appeared on Shofiq's face.

'Yes,' he said. 'All right.'

They went to face the music.